DO N **B**
BEGINNING TO END!

Are you s-s-s-scared of snakes?

Then don't buy the magic snake eyes at the gift shop in Lonestar National Park. True, they'll turn you into some cool animals. But the original owner wants them back. And he's one angry old rattlesnake!

You could get a map of a gold mine instead. You might strike it rich. On the other hand, you might end up dead. And that would make it hard to get your money back.

This is *your* camping trip. So you decide what will happen. And you decide how terrifying the scares will be!

Start on *PAGE 1*. Then follow the instructions at the bottom of each page. You make the choices. You can hunt for treasure, or fly high in the sky. But if you choose wrong, this camping trip is going to end very, very badly.

NOW, TAKE A DEEP BREATH. CROSS YOUR FINGERS, ARMS, TOES, AND LEGS. AND TURN TO *PAGE 1* TO *GIVE YOURSELF GOOSEBUMPS!*

READER BEWARE —
YOU CHOOSE THE SCARE!

Look for more
GIVE YOURSELF GOOSEBUMPS adventures
from R.L. STINE:

#1 Escape from the Carnival of Horrors
#2 Tick Tock, You're Dead!
#3 Trapped in Bat Wing Hall
#4 The Deadly Experiments of Dr. Eeek
#5 Night in Werewolf Woods
#6 Beware of the Purple Peanut Butter
#7 Under the Magician's Spell
#8 The Curse of the Creeping Coffin
#9 The Knight in Screaming Armor
#10 Diary of a Mad Mummy
#11 Deep in the Jungle of Doom
#12 Welcome to the Wicked Wax Museum
#13 Scream of the Evil Genie
#14 The Creepy Creations of Professor Shock
#15 Please Don't Feed the Vampire!
#16 Secret Agent Grandma
#17 Little Comic Shop of Horrors
#18 Attack of the Beastly Baby-sitter
#19 Escape from Camp Run-for-Your-Life
#20 Toy Terror: Batteries Included
#21 The Twisted Tale of Tiki Island
#22 Return to the Carnival of Horrors
#23 Zapped in Space
#24 Lost in Stinkeye Swamp
#25 Shop Till You Drop . . . Dead!

R.L. STINE

GIVE YOURSELF

Goosebumps®

ALONE IN
SNAKEBITE CANYON

AN
APPLE
PAPERBACK

SCHOLASTIC INC.
New York Toronto London Auckland Sydney

A PARACHUTE PRESS BOOK

ISBN 0-590-39997-7

12 11 10 9 8 7 6 5 4 3 2 1   8 9/9 0 1 2 3/0

Printed in the U.S.A.   40

First Scholastic printing, March 1998

GRRRRRRRROWLLLLL!

"Quit it, Pete!" you yell at your older brother. "For the zillionth time — I *know* you're not a panther."

"I made you jump. Admit it!" Pete says.

You scowl. You *are* feeling a little jumpy, but not because of Pete. There's something creepy about this dusty Visitors Center shop. Or maybe it's just that you're carsick. The road through Lonestar National Park was bumpy and rutted.

"Anyway, there are no panthers around here anymore," you add. "It's full of rattlesnakes now. That's why people call it Snakebite Canyon — not *Panther* Canyon."

Pete shrugs and wanders over to your parents. They're stocking up on camping supplies.

You're beginning to wonder if spending an entire week in this park is such a great idea. Then you glance into a dusty old glass display case. Awesome! It's filled with snake skulls, *real* Indian arrowheads, and cool-looking rocks.

In the middle of the case is a hairless old head. The skin is cracked and wrinkled all over. It looks mummified! It must be about a thousand years old.

The head grins. "Can I help you?" it asks.

Get ahead on PAGE 2.

2

You gasp.

Then the head rises. It's not a mummy head after all — it's just the old shopkeeper. He was staring at you from the other side of the glass case.

"Scared of wild animals, are you?" The shopkeeper cackles. "I have something that might help."

He holds out a box with a pair of little balls inside. They look like marbles.

"These are snake eyes." He winks. "*Magic* snake eyes!"

"Right," you murmur with a weak grin.

The old guy is crazy!

You're about to turn away when you glance at the snake eyes again.

They're glowing!

Go to PAGE 3.

Whoa! Maybe the snake eyes really *are* magic.

"The Quezot Indians knew how to use these magic eyes," the shopkeeper goes on. "You just rub them and — poof! You turn into an animal! Say a bear is chasing you. Why, you just rub the eyes, turn into a bird, and fly away. The transformation lasts for a thousand heartbeats. Long enough to make your escape."

You're thinking that sounds like a pretty good idea. You're sort of scared of bears.

Besides, wouldn't it be cool if the eyes really worked?

You just might buy them after all!

Then you notice the price tag.

It's almost all the money you've got!

Are they worth it?

While you try to decide, go to PAGE 4.

"Uh — they're a little expensive," you mumble.

The old man shrugs. "Well, how about a magic map, then?"

He points at an old paper scroll in the display case. The label says, MAP OF THE LOST GOLD MINE.

Wait a second! "How can the mine be lost?" you protest. "It's right on that map!"

The old man bends toward you. "That's not why it's called 'lost,'" he whispers. "It's called 'lost' because no one who's gone in there has ever come out again."

You swallow hard. "Really?"

"Really." He nods. "It's guarded by ancient magic. But they say there's enough gold piled up in the mine to buy this whole state. *If* you can pass all the magic tests."

Hmmm.

A gold mine protected by ancient magic.

Or a pair of snake eyes that turns humans into animals.

You don't have enough money to buy both.

Which would you rather have?

If you buy the snake eyes, turn to PAGE 26.
If you'd rather have the map, go to PAGE 77.

You scan the room with your eyes — and notice a big old wooden chest shoved against the wall. A treasure chest!

Hey! There's a keyhole in the top of the chest.

The panther growls. Your eyes dart back to the animal.

And you notice the keyhole in its golden collar.

"Uh-oh!" You poke Pete. "Look! There are *two* keyholes! Do I use the key to unlock the panther's collar — or to unlock the treasure chest?"

"That's a no-brainer," Pete declares. "The chest!"

You frown. "It seems too easy. What if this is another test? Maybe that chest is full of junk. Maybe I'm supposed to unlock the panther! Then it will disappear or something, and we'll get all the gold!"

"Or it will attack us," Pete argues. "Duhhh!"

You sigh. Maybe Pete is right. Maybe you should play it safe.

But you only have one chance at the gold!

To use the key on the chest, turn to PAGE 67.
To use it on the panther's collar, go to PAGE 25.

"I'm going," Pete announces. He starts climbing straight to the entrance.

After a minute, you follow him. It *is* shorter.

The climb is really hard. You have to pull yourself over some big rocks. But it's sort of fun too.

"Yaaaagghh!" Pete suddenly lets out a scream.

You glance up and spot your brother leaping down the mountain. He looks panicked. And you can see why.

A mountain lion is chasing him!

"Don't worry, Pete!" you shout.

Your guidebook says you can scare a mountain lion away. You just have to act as if you're going to attack *him*.

Or, on the other hand, you could run.

Think fast!

The mountain lion — and Pete — are about two leaps away from crashing right into you!

To try and scare off the lion, turn to PAGE 91.
To run, turn to PAGE 16.

Pete leans over your shoulder. A chill runs down your spine as he reads out loud:

WARNING! DANGER AWAITS YOU IF YOU ENTER THE GOLDEN CHAMBER WITHOUT THE GOLDEN KEY. IF YOU HAVE THE KEY — CONGRATULATIONS! BUT USE IT WISELY. OR ELSE YOU'LL BE VERY SORRY — FOR A VERY LONG TIME.

You gulp. Use it wisely? What does that mean?

"This is so cool!" Pete punches your shoulder. "You have the key! Oh, man, we're going to be rich!"

Your palms start to sweat. All that gold . . .

You can have anything you want. All your friends can have anything *they* want!

But what about the rest of the warning? That bit about using the key wisely, or else . . . ?

To learn more, go to PAGE 5.

I want to be a bird! you think.

You rub the glass eye showing the falcon.

A strange tingling starts in your stomach. Soon you feel itchy all over. Maybe this wasn't such a good idea!

You look down and see why you're itching. There are feathers sprouting out of your body! And you're shrinking!

Your jeans and pajamas fall off. You watch your feet turn into claws.

Maybe this wasn't such a good idea after all!

You try to scream for help. But the sound that comes out is a screech. And it's coming out of your *beak*.

You're a falcon!

This has to be a dream, you realize. You try to pinch yourself. But you flap your wing instead. It's no dream.

You remember something else the storekeeper said: "If you lose the snake eyes, you can't change back into a person."

You scoop up the eyes in your sharp beak.

You peer down at your feathered falcon's body. You know what you are going to do next.

You're going to fly!

Soar to PAGE 131.

You head for shore. Now that you're past the rapids, it's easier to swim. Soon you're in the shallows right near a riverbank.

Then your stomach rumbles again.

You feel feathers sprouting from your scales! At least let me be turning into a duck, you think.

You splash toward the shore, half-bird, half-fish. You barely make it before the change is complete.

You glance down at yourself. Hey. You're an owl! A wet owl.

You start to flap your wings and lift into the air.

Phew! It's good to be flying. And owls have great vision! From up here, you can see your camp. You race toward it.

Not far from camp, you start to feel funny. But it's not your stomach rumbling. Maybe a thousand heartbeats are up.

You think you can land at camp before you change. But then you spot an early-morning tour group. Maybe you should change back to your own shape right in front of them.

That would give them a shock!

Or should you just land at your tent?

Scare the tourists on PAGE 60.
Land out of sight on PAGE 124.

10

You check out the map. A whole new section seems to jump out at you!

What is with this map?

Now it shows a short trail that neatly avoids the worst of the canyons.

"The trail looks pretty easy," you tell Pete in relief. "We should be there in about fifteen minutes!"

An hour later, you stop for another rest. "We should have taken the bus!" Pete gasps, fanning himself with his hands.

You wipe sweat off your forehead. Actually, you think, it's been an easy hike. *Too* easy. You haven't gotten lost. Not once. You haven't even stumbled or stubbed your toe! And you're not the world's best hiker.

You have a bad feeling. A very bad feeling.

You shake your head impatiently. You're being dumb!

"Let's keep going," you tell Pete. "It's worth the hike. Don't forget, we'll have a ton of gold soon!"

At last you reach the mountain. The map changes again. It shows an easy climb to the mine entrance.

Two minutes later, you're there. Just like that.

"We did it!" Pete crows. "We found the Lost Mine!"

Now, can you find PAGE 126?

"I'll show you who's chicken!" you growl.

You find a nice, thick stick. You test the trap by shoving the stick into the jaws.

SNAP! A couple of inches disappear off the end of the stick. The jaws reset pretty quickly. But Pete's right — there *is* time to make it.

You back up the mine shaft. Then you run toward the trap with the stick held out in front of you.

At the last minute, you jump.

But, like Pete says, it's all a matter of timing. . . .

Will you make it? Look at a clock, right now!

If the minutes on the clock are even, turn to PAGE 119.

If the minutes are odd, turn to PAGE 29.

You've always wanted to be a spelunker. That's someone who explores caves. With bat senses, you'll be the best spelunker ever!

You rub the snake eye showing the bat. You gasp as your skin stretches from your fingertips to your sides to make a wing.

Then your chest and your face get furry. It tickles!

When the transformation is over, you pick up the snake eyes in your bat feet. And flap into the cave.

As you fly along, you hear yourself making little cheeping noises. The noises bounce off the walls of the cave. Then your bat brain turns the echoes into a picture of the cave.

Awesome!

You can see with your ears!

With your new sonar, you detect an insect flying in front of you. Without thinking, you swerve toward it. You catch the bug in your mouth. Mmmmm. It's a crunchy, tasty mosquito. . . .

Mosquito?

EEEEEWWWW! You just ate a mosquito!

Flit to PAGE 15.

You inch around the corner. You poke your head into the Golden Chamber.

You gulp. The room is stuffed with gold! Gold bars! Gold bricks! Gold coins!

But crouched on top of that huge, glowing stack of gold is a big black cat. Wearing a golden collar.

A panther!

Pete stands frozen in the entrance, staring at the cat.

"Pete," you whisper. "Back away — slowly!"

Pete takes one step backwards.

Then he turns and bolts from the room.

The panther snarls, bares gleaming fangs — and leaps!

Its razor-sharp claws reach out as it hurtles straight toward — you!

Turn to PAGE 123.

14

It's your brother, Pete!

"Aaaaaah!" he yells. "You scared me!"

"You scared *me*!" you yell back. "What are you doing here?"

Pete shuffles his feet. "Some old guy at the gift shop sold me a map. He said this mine has lots of gold in it!"

"And you didn't tell me?" you shriek. "Some brother."

"Yeah? Well, you followed me!" he accuses.

"No, I didn't! The snake eyes started glowing, and I turned into a falcon and a bat and took a ride in a railroad car . . . "

Pete glares at you like you're crazy. "Yeah, sure!"

"Well, at least you've got a map. Let me see it."

Pete hands you the old map. It's kind of blurry. Strangely, reading it gives you a headache. The only part that's clear is the word WARNING near the bottom. But the words under it swim before your eyes.

"This map is creepy," you declare.

But Pete is staring right past you. "You think the map's creepy . . . look at that!"

You turn. Something glimmers through the dimness.

Something big.

Go to PAGE 58.

And the grossest thing is, that mosquito tasted *good*!

You flap through the cave, dodging the sharp stalactites that drip from the ceiling.

Then your stomach tingles. The snake eyes are wearing off!

Seconds later, you land on the ground with a *THUNK*.

"Owww!" you cry. That hurt! And you can't see a thing in the black cave. Without bat sonar, you're blind.

But you can still hear sounds. Dripping water, the flutter of wings. And something else. From far down the tunnel . . . a rattle.

It sounds like a rattlesnake!

You think of the legend. About how the angry snake is still searching for its eyes.

But that's just a dumb story.

You hear the rattle again. This time it's closer.

You gulp. You have to stay calm. There are lots of rattlesnakes at Big Bend, you tell yourself. Perfectly *normal* rattlesnakes.

Ummm. Maybe you should get out of here, after all.

Grope your way to PAGE 44.

"Run, Pete!" you scream.

That lion doesn't look easy to scare!

You turn and jump down to the next rock. Your sneakers almost slip. Why didn't you buy real climbing shoes?

"Wait for me!" Pete yells. He leaps across a wide space between two rocks.

Your heart stands still, but he lands perfectly.

"You're a natural-born climber," you tell him.

"Not as natural as that lion!" Pete pants. He jumps again. You're right on his heels, hurtling from rock to rock.

"We're going to make it, Pete!" you yell breathlessly.

"Yeah, we're" — Pete suddenly slips and loses his balance—"Whoaaa!" he yells.

Pete crashes into you. You both fall, skidding down the loose rocks of the slope.

A snarl sounds right above you. You peer up — into the open mouth of one hungry-looking mountain lion.

So much for shortcuts.

Now you and Pete are *cold* cuts!

THE END

You shake your head. It's just a dumb story.

About a mean, blind rattlesnake.

That hangs around the area where you happen to be camping with your family.

Looking for the person who has its eyes.

When you get into your sleeping bag that night, you make sure it's *completely* empty . . . not because of the legend, or anything. It's just common sense to do that when you're camping in the wilderness. Yeah. That's it.

A little while later, Pete's snores are so loud, they wake you. You sit up. And your eyes widen with surprise.

Something is glowing near your feet. It's coming from your jeans, which are folded and lying on your pack.

The snake eyes!

The glow is showing clear through the pocket.

You wriggle into the jeans and roll out of the small tent. You pull the snake eyes from your pocket. They're hot, like marbles left in the sun.

You hold one up to your eye for a closer look.

And you can't believe what you see!

Take a closer look on PAGE 86.

You whirl around.

It's the old Indian woman who told you the way to the chapel. "I warned you — don't bother the ghosts!" She cackles. "You must be a lucky one. You're still alive — for now!"

She walks away laughing. Pete runs up.

"All right! You made it!" he cries. "I knew you could outrun that old hunk of junk."

You smile. Then you remember to be mad at him.

"You left me to get speared!" you complain. "This wouldn't have happened if we followed the Lost Mine Trail like I wanted."

"That's not the way I see it," Pete argues.

"Oh, yeah?" You stomp over to the bus stop. "Well, it's my map. So from now on, we're doing things my way. And I say . . . "

What do you say? Find out on PAGE 49.

You decide to take the Watchers' test. After all, you've got to be smarter than a bunch of walking eyeballs!

"Ask me anything!" you command.

The Watchers form a line in front of you. The middle one announces, "We are the three Watchers. We always stand in a line, but not always in the same order."

The one on the right says, "I never stand next to the Watcher with the most eyeballs."

The one in the middle declares, "I always stand next to the Watcher with the second-most eyeballs."

"And I sometimes stand in the middle, and sometimes not," the one on the left tells you.

Together, they ask, "Which of us has the most eyeballs?"

"Huh?" You gulp and glance at Pete. But he's staring at the Watchers in a kind of trance of horror.

You're on your own. Concentrate!

The one on the right said he never stands next to the Watcher with the most eyeballs. And he's standing next to the one in the middle. So it *can't* be the one in the middle.

But which of the other two is it?

If you think it's the one on the left, go to PAGE 59.

If you think it's the one on the right, go to PAGE 128.

You rub the mosquito snake eye. You don't want to be an insect — and you don't know how you're going to change back. You'll be too small to carry the snake eyes with you.

But right now, all you can think about is getting out of this cave — and away from that horrible rattlesnake!

You feel yourself growing smaller and smaller. New legs sprout out of your bug body. You have three pairs of them now.

You peer at your wings in the dim light. There are *four* of those. You take off.

Wow! Being a mosquito is almost cooler than being a falcon. You can hover in place — like a helicopter!

You whiz around, testing your new flying abilities. Then you hear a cute cheeping sound. Maybe it's another mosquito. You could have a little mosquito friend!

The cheeping sound gets closer. It's a familiar sound. It's the sound of . . . a bat!

Uh-oh. You remember how much bats like the taste of mosquitoes. From personal experience.

You buzz toward the hole in the roof. The cheeps get louder. The bat gets closer. You can hear its leathery wings flapping.

But you can't get away.

Doesn't that bug you?

THE END

"I can't see a thing!" Pete complains.

"No kidding," you mutter. Your stomach knots up.

You feel your way along the wall. It's clammy. Ugh! But you remind yourself that being cold and scared won't matter — not when you find all that gold.

Then you see a faint glow ahead.

"That way," you tell Pete. You stumble toward the glow.

The rumbling noise grows louder.

What *is* it? you wonder uneasily.

You and Pete hurry around a sharp bend in the tunnel. The glow is suddenly blindingly bright. Golden light spills out of a doorway carved in the rock.

The Golden Chamber?

The rumbling sounds like thunder now.

What are you going to see in there?

Find out on PAGE 13!

22

You decide to become a flying squirrel. You rub the snake eye, and a tingling feeling comes over you. The branch you're clinging to is getting bigger.

No, you're getting smaller!

Fur sprouts all over your body. You watch wide-eyed as flaps of skin unfold from your sides. They're almost like little furry wings!

Just before your hands turn into paws, you remember to pop the snake eyes into your mouth.

The bees stop swarming around you. Maybe you're too small for them to worry about. Or maybe they know squirrels don't like honey.

But then the snake rattles below you. You glance down.

That snake looks *much* bigger when you're a squirrel.

Time to fly.

You squint again at your fuzzy "wings." You sure hope they work. You step to the edge of the branch. The nearest tree is pretty far away. And it's a long way down.

Oh, well, here goes nothing.

You jump . . .

And you're falling toward the snake. Way too fast!

Fall all the way down to PAGE 129.

"Find something sharp!" you scream. "Cut off my sleeve!"

Pete scrambles from one side of the tunnel to the other.

By now the grinding teeth have pulled in almost all the fabric of your sleeve.

It's like being stuck in some giant sewing machine that's sucking you in — in slow motion!

"I can't find anything," Pete yells. He trips over the railroad track.

That gives you an idea.

"Pete, pull up a spike from the railroad ties!"

"What?" Pete asks.

He can be so dense! "The boards between the metal rails," you explain. "They have long nails in them. Pull one out!"

Metal scrapes against your bare flesh. "My arm," you whimper. You wish you never came into this dumb mine!

You hear Pete grunting as he pulls at the tracks. Then he flies backwards as a spike comes free. "Got one!"

"Owwww!" you moan. The metal teeth scrape harder against your flesh.

You swallow hard. The next bite will be a bad one.

Quick! Sink your teeth into PAGE 79.

You decide to go along with Pete. If you can see the entrance shining in the sun, you have a better chance of finding the mine — and the gold!

You and Pete quickly make some sandwiches. You leave a note for your parents: GONE HIKING.

The town of San Vicente isn't far away. A rusty bus takes you there. You ask a few people where the old chapel is. But, strangely, nobody will answer you.

"We can't give up. What should we do?" you ask Pete.

"I will help you!"

You turn. An old Indian woman smiles at you. She points to a crooked, narrow street. "The chapel is down there. But don't go inside!" she warns. "You'll disturb the ghosts!"

You feel a chill. But Pete snickers. "Ghosts?"

You thank the old lady and pull Pete away. You find the old chapel — a falling-down ruin. You stand in the entrance.

"It's right before dawn," you declare. "We'll see the sun's reflection in a minute."

You can almost feel the gold in your hands!

Then a low moan comes from the chapel.

You jump. "It's a ghost!" you whisper.

Turn to PAGE 71.

You step cautiously toward the panther. It lifts its head, revealing the keyhole. You fit the key in. *CLICK!*

You gasp as the key dissolves in your hand. There's a burst of blinding, golden light.

A laugh echoes through the chamber. An evil laugh. "Thanks for replacing me!" a throaty voice murmurs.

Huh?

The light gets so bright, it hurts. You throw your hands over your eyes. Then the light disappears.

So does the panther.

"Pete!" you croak. You can hardly talk.

Because now the golden collar is fastened around *your* neck. It's locked tight — and there's no more key!

"Pete — get help!" you manage to say. "Bring a locksmith!"

Pete tears off down the tunnel. The sound of his footsteps fades into silence.

Then you realize — he forgot to take the map!

Without it, he'll never find his way back to the mine — or the Golden Chamber!

Which means you're going to be enjoying all that gold for a long time. A *very* long time!

THE END

You decide to buy the snake eyes. They probably don't work, but they look so cool.

Outside, you show the box to Pete.

"I hope you got some snake eyes of your own," you say with a smirk.

"Snake eyes? What for?"

You take off the lid. "They're magic. So when a big bear comes into our camp tonight, I'm going to turn into a bird and fly away. *You're* going to be bear food."

"Magic eyes? Yeah, right." Pete snorts.

You hold up the eyes. "Look, they're glowing!"

"That's just the sun, stupid," Pete argues.

You inspect the eyes more closely. Well, they *were* glowing before. Weren't they?

Then you see a piece of paper folded up tightly in the box. You open it. It's covered with tiny writing. You can hardly read it.

You scan the first words. And a chill goes down your spine.

Read them on PAGE 135.

"Pete!" you scream. "Go back and get the ore car!"

"Right." Pete runs into the darkness.

The teeth press closer to your arm. You feel as if you're caught by a giant bulldog who won't let go.

"Pete!" you call. "Hurry!"

There's no answer.

You've got to slow down the trap!

Hmmm. Maybe if you stick a rock between the teeth, they'll jam. With your foot, you roll a rock toward you. You use your other foot to balance it on top of your shoe.

You give a little kick. The rock flies into the air.

You grab for it with your free hand.

You caught it!

You shove the rock between the metal teeth.

The trap lets out a hideous wail. Maybe you've broken it!

But the stone is quickly ground to dust.

Then you hear something squeaking toward you. It sounds like an army of mice. Or a rusty old ore car!

Pete bursts from the gloom. He's pushing the car ahead of him at about a hundred miles an hour. It's headed right for the trap!

Unfortunately, it's also headed right for you.

Head to PAGE 105.

You're good at talking — to people. Ghosts can't be too different, right?

"We c-c-came to find the Lost Mine," you stutter. Your voice comes out high and squeaky.

The armor clanks as the spear floats closer to your throat. You swallow hard. The point of the spear brushes your neck.

"*We* found the mine," the ghost tells you. "Four hundred years ago. It was rich with gold. Every shovelful of dirt was worth a fortune! We stored our treasure in the Golden Chamber."

You wonder why he's telling you all this.

"The Quezot Indians lived here then," the ghost continues. "They were weak. We made them our slaves. They dug our gold for us. Then one day, they rebelled — and killed us all."

"Serves you right," you murmur.

Pete gives you a look that says "shut up!"

"The Quezot put spells on all the mine entrances. Spells to keep people out." The ghost pauses. "But there is a secret entrance. One the Quezot knew nothing about."

The ghost pulls a lever. Torches hanging on the wall suddenly burst into flame!

Turn to PAGE 93.

You sail toward the jaws, keeping your eyes shut.

SNAP!

Your breath is knocked out of you as you hit the ground. You're afraid to open your eyes. With one hand, you feel your head, legs, arms . . .

Everything is still there.

You made it!

"Not bad," Pete comments. "Even though I showed you how to do it."

"Right," you mutter. "Just follow me, okay? We still have to find the gold. Or did you forget why we're here?"

Holding the glowing key as a torch, you and Pete inch down the mine shaft. Ahead, you hear a faint rumbling sound.

"It sounds like some kind of engine," you whisper.

"Not an engine," Pete argues. "Something else. Not mechanical." He snaps his fingers. "I know! A purring cat."

"No way! It would have to be a *huge* cat," you argue.

Just then, the glowing key flickers like a candle.

And winks out.

It's dark. Really dark.

Grope your way to PAGE 21.

Maybe scaring Pete wasn't such a good idea. The ranger looks like she means business.

You try to talk to her, but it just comes out as a big, nasty growl. She raises the tranquilizer gun.

Okay, so talking didn't work. But actions speak louder than words. You back away from her. You sit back on your haunches and raise your paws.

Nice ranger?

The ranger lowers her gun and stares at you. Hey! Maybe this will work.

If you can communicate with her, everything will be all right. On the other hand, your communication skills are limited. And the ranger might get scared and shoot you.

Maybe it's time to head for the hills.

What will you do? Try to communicate? Or run like crazy?

Try to communicate with the ranger on PAGE 65.

Or run like a crazy bear to PAGE 96.

You shut your eyes, waiting for something horrible to happen.

But the spear doesn't pierce your flesh. Instead, the terrible laughter dies away. There's empty silence around you.

You slowly open your eyes and peer around.

There's nothing left of the ghost. No armor, no spear. Only a pile of small, silvery slivers on the dusty ground.

A ray of light blinds you. Squinting, you realize that the sun has come up.

"Dawn," you whisper. "The ghost must have been destroyed by the dawn!"

You struggle to your feet. You're feeling pretty shaky.

You feel even shakier when a hideous laugh breaks out behind you!

Find out what's so funny on PAGE 18.

You rub the eye, feeling a little bit silly as you do.

Then you start to feel itchy. You scratch your skin, but the itching gets worse.

Then you let out a gasp. Long black hairs are growing all over you! This is kind of scary. You're not sure if you like it.

And you're getting much, *much* bigger. Your jeans are too tight, all of a sudden. You struggle out of them. Your hands are turning into claws too. *Bear* claws!

You decide you *do* like this.

Standing upright is getting hard, though. You let yourself fall forward onto all fours.

Going around on all fours is easy as pie when you're a bear.

Speaking of pie, you can smell some! You can smell the food that your family brought, and all the other food at the campsite.

You follow your nose to the pie smell. Rats! It's in one of those bearproof boxes. You shake one, but it holds firm.

A voice from inside your tent whispers, "Is that you?"

It's Pete! You must have woken him up!

Turn to PAGE 41.

You snatch the paper from Pete's hand.

Pete shakes his head. "No kidding there's a price. How much did you pay for those eyes, sucker?"

"I think they're cool," you mutter. You fold up the paper and tuck it into your pocket.

Just then your mom walks up.

"Ready, campers?" she asks.

You all climb into the car and head for the campsite.

You're staying in the Quezot basin. There are picnic tables, cooking grills, and metal boxes where you can lock up your food. The boxes are marked BEARPROOF. Awesome!

You and Pete set up the tent you'll be sharing. The minute he wanders off to look for firewood, you crawl inside. You unfold the paper that came with the snake eyes, and keep reading.

"Legend says the rattlesnake still searches for its eyes. It roams the Quezot basin and hills. And it burns with anger, planning a terrible revenge on the thief who has its eyes."

The thief who has its eyes? you think.

That would be *me*.

Turn to PAGE 17.

You decide to fly away.

And it's a good thing. One of the rafters screams and swings his paddle at you.

You flap your wings and soar down the river.

You glance at your reflection in the water. You're an owl!

You fly high above the boat. The rafters are staring at you, as if they still can't believe their eyes.

You fly even higher and gaze around. From up here, you can see your campsite! You head toward it, as fast as you can. You don't want your stomach to start rumbling while you're in midair.

Just as you get to the camp, you start to feel the change again. But your stomach didn't rumble.

Maybe your thousand heartbeats are up.

You figure you can just make it to your tent. You can't wait to crawl into your sleeping bag and take a nap.

Then you see a group of hikers on a nearby trail.

You could land and change back into a human right in front of them. What an awesome trick!

Scare the tourists on PAGE 60.
Land near your tent on PAGE 124.

You rub the snake eye showing the mountain lion. Your stomach gurgles. Then your arms grow longer. Golden hair slides out of them. You feel fangs sprouting from your gums. You test them with your tongue. They're sharp!

You pop the snake eyes under your tongue.

Then you open your mouth and let out a practice growl.

"GRRRRRR!"

A flock of small birds on the rocks below takes off quickly. Two rabbits scuttle under some bushes.

You are the king of the desert! You rule all the other animals.

Then you hear a rattling noise. Somewhere down in the rocks lurks a rattlesnake.

But you're a big mountain lion! You're not afraid of some dinky snake.

Then you remember the last words of the snake eyes legend.

"The rattlesnake still searches for its eyes . . . and it burns with anger, planning a terrible revenge on the thief who has its eyes."

The rattle comes from the rocks again.

It sounds even closer. Too close for comfort.

Turn to PAGE 134.

"Wait!" you cry. You bend down, holding the key close to the teeth. They're so big, they're blocking the tunnel.

"It looks like an old bear trap," you tell Pete.

Wow. Most traps just clamp on to an animal's ankle. But this one could snap you in half.

A message is carved in the rock wall beside it:

THE WAY TO THE GOLDEN CHAMBER IS DOWN
MY THROAT.

You bet the Golden Chamber is where the gold is. But you'll have to go through the trap to get there!

Cautiously, you bend closer.

SNAP! The jaws swing shut an inch from your nose. Then, with a screech of rusty metal, the trap opens again!

"It resets itself," you murmur. "Whoa!"

Pete picks up a long stick from the tunnel floor. "Let's throw this into it. We can jump past when the teeth are shut."

You frown. "Are you sure?"

"Watch." Pete charges toward the jaws with the stick in front of him. Just before he reaches the trap, he ducks and rolls — right toward the huge, pointy teeth.

"Pete!" you scream.

SNAP!

The dust settles on PAGE 111.

You dive for the river.

As you speed toward it, you feel your wings turning back into arms. Your feathers are falling out!

By the time you are over the river, you're not flying anymore. Just falling. You tumble out of the sky and smack against the water. Ouch!

Everything goes silent as you plunge underwater. Then you struggle to the surface. You pop up, coughing and gasping.

You shake the water out of your eyes and glance around. High canyon walls rise up on both sides. The cold river rushes you downstream. It's a good thing you can swim.

Then you hear a loud, roaring sound. The current picks up speed.

As you round a canyon wall, you gasp. Just ahead are the worst rapids you've ever seen. Jagged rocks rise out of boiling, white water. And you're rushing toward them like a freight train!

Swim to PAGE 74.

HSSSSSS! The spider shoots more web at you.

But this time, the web isn't coming out straight. It's falling all over the spider!

The spider makes a horrible screeching sound. But the noise is oddly muffled — as if its mouth is full of peanut butter!

Then the spider lurches toward you — but falls, tangled in its own web! You can't let this chance pass.

"Come on!" You grab Pete and race down the tunnel.

"Oh, no!" Pete suddenly cries.

The way is blocked by a wall of rocks!

"Dig!" you pant.

You and Pete heave boulders out of the way. Soon you scoop out a hole big enough to squeeze through. Golden light shines out of the hole.

You scramble through — and drop into a big, cavelike room.

A room piled high with gold!

You pull out the map. "It must be the Golden Chamber!"

"Yeah. But what's that sound?" Pete whispers.

You listen. A deep humming fills the air.

Weird. It sounds almost like purring.

And then you see two big green cat eyes, staring straight at you.

Meet the kitty on PAGE 76.

Go down a tunnel that's not even on the map? No thanks.

You roll up the map and grab Pete's hand. Together, you start backing toward the stairs. "Uh, we have a sunrise we wanted to catch," you babble. "So I guess we'll be going now."

"Thanks for the help, though," Pete chimes in.

The ghost lifts his spear. "If you won't claim the gold, then you can help guard it!"

You turn to run, but suddenly your muscles lock.

You glance at Pete. He can't move, either!

What have they done to you?

"These two will make fine guards," one ghost groans.

"When they become ghosts," another adds.

The floating spears are raised all around you. The ghosts herd you and Pete into a corner.

"Careful!" You gulp. "Those spears are sharp!"

The ghosts laugh hollowly. "We know," they answer.

Pete whimpers beside you. You know how he feels!

You and Pete huddle closer together. Your mind is racing. Maybe you can still get away. Maybe you can think of a plan.

But deep down, you know better. You and Pete don't have the ghost of a chance. Sorry, but this is really

THE END.

40

You manage to grab the rock with your finger-nails and haul yourself up.

You rub your hands. Ow! That hurts when you're not a mountain lion!

The desert is just below. You climb gingerly down the rocks, wishing that a thousand heart-beats lasted just a little longer.

When you're on solid ground, you scan the area. It's a scrubby, flat desert — just like in the movies, but hotter. Much hotter. Heat waves roll off the brown sand and rocks.

This looks bad. You don't have any water. You don't even have any clothes! And there's no way you can climb back up that mountain.

Worse, the snake is still following you.

Behind you in the rocks, you hear the rattling again. The wind picks up. It sounds almost like a voice. And it's calling, *"Give me back my eyesssss. . . ."*

A chill runs down your spine. You're starting to understand something.

If the snake eyes work, then maybe the legend about them is true. That means the snake that's following you is highly *annoyed*. After all, you've got its eyes.

Turn to PAGE 97.

Oh, no!

If Pete sees you now, he's going to scream his head off and wake everyone up.

On the other hand, he laughed at your snake eyes.

One roar could give Pete a pretty good scare. He deserves it, after all. You'd definitely get the last laugh.

What'll it be?

Scare Pete on PAGE 104.
Or sneak away to PAGE 73.

You choose the left-hand panel. You push against it — and it slides open!

"It's empty!" You slump in disappointment.

"You doofus!" Pete yells. "The line on the right *was* longer! I told you!"

You quickly reach for the right-hand panel. Too late!

A metal gate slides over it, almost catching your fingers.

"Now what do we do?" you ask.

"Well, we have to go in," Pete points out. "Key or no key."

He's right. So you walk through the yawning entrance.

It's pitch-black inside the mine. You wish you'd brought flashlights.

You find an old railroad track. You follow it deep into a long, narrow tunnel. Then you stumble over something big.

"It's an old ore car!" Pete exclaims. "Miners used these to cart dirt out of the mines."

"Dirt — and gold," you state. "We must be getting closer to the treasure!"

Pete pokes you. "Hey, I think I see something up there!"

You squint into the darkness.

And gasp in horror.

Take a chilling look at PAGE 58.

You can't let Pete explore the chapel alone. Or with a ghost.

You cross your fingers and follow him inside.

The chapel smells old and musty, even with the desert wind coming straight through the empty windows. Every step throws up a little cloud of dust. The big room is shrouded in deep shadows.

"Pete?" you call in a low voice.

Pete doesn't answer. Instead, another moan echoes through the room. You jump about a foot.

You consider heading back outside. You wish you could run. But you have to find Pete. You swallow.

You feel your way along the chapel wall. You follow some stairs down to cool darkness. The walls here are dirt.

It's like you're walking into . . . a grave.

Then you hear the moan again, right in front of you.

And another sound too — clanking metal.

Heading right toward you!

Go to PAGE 82.

But first you have to find the snake eyes.

You skim your hands over the ground until you feel them. As you scoop up the eyes, your hand brushes against something metal.

You try to pick it up. It won't budge. It feels as if it's nailed to the floor.

You grope your hand down the piece of metal, feeling for the end. It's really long. In fact, it seems to go on forever.

Then you realize what it is. You know that miners used trainlike cars to carry ore out of the mines. It's a track for an ore car! This cave must lead into an old mine.

You hear the rattling noise again.

Time to get going!

You start shuffling along. After a few steps, you bump into something. You reach out and run your hands down the object. It's a box on wheels. It must be an ore car. Maybe you can ride it out of the cave.

You give the car a push, but it's stuck. Should you take the time to fix it? Or should you just keep walking — to put as much space between you and that rattling noise as possible!

To take a ride on the railroad, turn to PAGE 55.
To keep walking, turn to PAGE 47.

Just as the hairy legs reach out, you manage to drag yourself and Pete into the secret passage.

The wall slides shut, blocking off the spider.

Safe! You take a few deep breaths to calm down. Pete is stamping his feet, trying to knock off the spider goo.

"You shouldn't have made it mad," he complains.

"Things could have been a lot worse," you snap back.

Some thanks you get for saving him!

There aren't any torches in this tunnel. It's too dark to see, so you have to feel your way along the clammy walls.

Pete keeps one hand on your arm as you inch forward.

"Ouch!" You stumble and throw out your hands to stop your fall. You land on metal — long tracks of metal with pieces of wood linking them together. A small wooden cart sits on the tracks.

"Hey! It's an old railroad track. That's an ore car!" You feel a burst of excitement. "This really is the Lost Mine! Gold, here we come!"

Your voice echoes strangely, bouncing off the walls. The sound gives you the creeps, but you're too excited to care. You hurry along the tracks.

"I see gold!" Pete points to a faint glimmer ahead.

Your heart leaps. Until you see what it *really* is.

Take a look on PAGE 58.

This is terrible! Your name is too long!

Didn't it ever occur to your parents that you might turn into a bear and have to scratch your name in the dirt?

It's taking forever to write the letters with your clumsy bear paw. Before you get very far, two more rangers jump out of their truck.

One of them raises another tranquilizer gun.

You lift your paw and try to yell, "Wait!"

Ooops.

It comes out as a nasty growl. Both rangers fire. You feel little pinpricks as the tranquilizer darts sink in. Uh-oh.

At first, you just feel sleepy. Not so bad.

Then you notice the little glowing snake eyes on the ground by your tent. What did the store-keeper say? Oh, yeah, don't lose them or you won't be able to change back into a person.

You walk toward the eyes, but you feel as if you weigh a thousand pounds. Then you think, I *do* weigh a thousand pounds.

Just before you reach the snake eyes, you collapse. You gaze at them through heavy eyes. There was a reason you wanted them. But you can't seem to remember it.

Oh, well, it'll come back to you after a good night's sleep.

Wake up on PAGE 99.

You shuffle along the train track for what seems like hours.

Then you blink. Is that light ahead? You rush toward it.

The light pours from a hole in the cave ceiling. High in the ceiling. There's no way you can climb up there.

The rattling sound echoes through the cave behind you. Now you're positive. It's *definitely* a rattlesnake.

Your hand holding the snake eyes grows warm. You look down and see that the snake eyes are glowing again.

In one of them, you see a spider. It's big and gray and furry. A tarantula.

With a shudder, you peer at the other snake eye.

This one shows a mosquito flitting around.

As a mosquito, you could fly up to the hole in the roof. But how would you carry the snake eyes?

As a tarantula, you could climb up with the eyes in your mouth. But it will take you forever.

You jump when you hear the rattle again. The snake is much closer. You've got to get out of this cave!

Quick. What's it going to be?

To become a mosquito, buzz to PAGE 20.
To become a tarantula, crawl to PAGE 51.

The bees swarm around you. You try to tell them that you don't want their honey. But all that comes out is a growl.

You wave your paws, but that angers the bees more. Then one stings you!

Ow! But it's not as bad as you thought. You've got thick bear skin and hair to protect you.

Your stomach suddenly lurches. Your body tingles. The hair on your arms is melting away. You're turning back into a human!

And the bees are still mad. Ouch! Right on the nose! That *really* hurt! You don't have thick bear hair anymore. You don't even have clothes on. You've gone from bear to bare!

Time to get out of here.

You spit the snake eyes into your hand and peer into them. One shows a flying squirrel. Unfortunately, you can't remember whether flying squirrels really fly. Maybe they just jump from tree to tree? The other eye shows a hummingbird. Is it big enough to carry the snake eyes?

You stare down at the snake. Its huge, thick body slithers up the tree. Its empty eye sockets seem to stare up at you.

Which eye will you rub?

To turn into a flying squirrel, glide to PAGE 22.
To turn into a hummingbird, flit off to PAGE 120.

"Well?" Pete prompts.

"I say we take the Lost Mine Trail!" you declare.

You and Pete hike the short distance to the trailhead. There's a big arrow and a sign: MINE TRAIL THIS WAY.

You head out. The trail starts off easy. Then it gets steep and tough.

Pete starts complaining.

"This trail stinks," he grumbles. "Why did they put a mine on top of a mountain, anyway?"

"Because that's where the gold was," you snap.

"Well, it's way too steep," Pete goes on. He kicks a rock.

A bunch of stones spills down the trail.

"Would you quit messing around?" you grumble.

"I didn't do that," Pete insists. "It came from farther up."

"Maybe it was a mountain lion," you suggest sarcastically.

Pete looks nervous. You're glad.

Then more rocks fall. And scrambling sounds echo around you. They seem to come from everywhere.

"It *is* a mountain lion! Let's beat it!" Pete yells.

Too late! A dark shape flies toward you from the rocks above.

Scramble to PAGE 64.

"I'm not chicken, I'm smart," you tell yourself as you search for another way to get past the trap.

You kneel out of range of the teeth. Maybe you can figure out how this thing works. You might be able to take it apart. You're pretty good at that kind of stuff.

"Bawk! Bawk! Bawk!" Pete teases, doing his chicken dance.

You wish he'd dance right into the trap.

Then you spot a little hole at the hinge of the trap.

A keyhole!

"Hey!" you shout. "I found a keyhole. This must be where we use the golden key!"

You carefully slide the key into place. It turns. . . .

With a terrible clanking, legs unfold beneath the teeth. The trap shakes off years of dust — and stands up!

It's become a huge metal monster. A monster that groans and screeches, sending a shiver up your spine.

It looks *alive*.

And it's walking. Right toward you!

Turn to PAGE 69.

You rub the tarantula snake eye, trying not to imagine how gross you're going to look. At least you'll get out of this cave.

Your stomach lurches, and you start shrinking. Fur pops out on your legs. All . . . four of them? Make that all six of them. Wait. Make that all eight of them.

Eight hairy legs. And you've got four pairs of eyes. Creepy!

You scoop up the snake eyes and crawl toward the cave wall. You can't move fast, but you can climb straight up the rock!

This is great! There's no way that snake can climb after you. You've escaped it for good.

You reach the hole in the ceiling, climb out, and glance around.

It's afternoon. You're next to a vast empty space. It's got giant, strange markings. Is it a football field? A parking lot?

You crawl onto it. Then you see headlights. Oh! It's a highway. And the headlights are on a big truck. A big truck heading straight toward you. Eeeeek!

You run back the way you came. But tarantulas run *really* slowly. The truck bears down on you.

Geez. Eight eyes, and you forgot to look both ways!

THE END

52

You decide to wait to see if the rafters will help you.

You're just sprouting your tail feathers when one of the rafters shouts, "It's a monster!"

Oh, no! You flap your wings. But another rafter swings a paddle. It hits your head. *BONK!*

The rafters seize you. One of them stuffs you into a canvas bag. Before you know what's going on, you drift into unconsciousness. . . .

When you wake up, you find yourself in a big cage. A lot of kids and adults are staring at you and pointing.

"Look, Mommy! It's waking up!" shouts a little girl with cotton candy smeared all over her face.

Oh, bummer. You're in a zoo!

Turn to PAGE 84.

You're in the water, so it makes sense to be a fish, you think.

You rub the wet snake eye. This better work. The rapids are coming up fast!

A tingly feeling washes over you. Your stomach gurgles. You pop the remaining snake eye into your mouth. You're *not* going to swallow this one!

Your arms grow scales and fold into your body. Your legs grow together into a tail.

As your head slips underwater, you hold your breath.

Then you realize you're a fish!

You take a tiny breath of water. Hmmmm. Not bad. Then another. Soon you're breathing as if you were born with gills.

You zoom into the rapids. You dodge rocks. You swoop through the swirling water. Your fins are like wings! You're the fighter plane of fish!

Your stomach starts gurgling again. Hey! It's too soon for you to change back.

Then you realize you haven't eaten breakfast. Dinner was a long time ago. You're just hungry.

Then your stomach rumbles again, and you feel funny.

Uh-oh! You *are* changing again!

Head to PAGE 88.

The ghost prods you with its spear.

"Right," you say. "We're dying to take the secret passage."

You grab Pete's arm. "Come on," you whisper. "The ghosts want us to find the gold."

"Or else they're lying to us," Pete whispers back.

You try not to think about that possibility. You have a terrible feeling that you don't really have a choice.

The tunnel stretches out before you. You're relieved that the ghosts don't follow. Their moaning dies away behind you.

"It's awfully quiet in here," Pete mutters.

Too quiet, you think. The only sounds are the sputtering of the torches — and your own footsteps. It gives you the creeps.

You step on something hard. You try to lift your foot to see what it is. But your foot feels stuck.

You glance down.

Yuck! The floor is covered with broken skeletons — skeletons covered with sticky goo!

Don't stick around here — check out PAGE 95.

You give the ore car a hard push. It budges an inch. You push again, and it bursts free from whatever was holding it. You jump in. After all, why walk when you can ride?

The car rattles along the tracks. You're headed downward. The car starts to pick up speed. You wonder if it has brakes!

Maybe you should have checked.

The car goes faster and faster, shaking so violently that it almost throws you out. Then you peer ahead — and scream!

The car is about to crash into a wall!

Keep riding to PAGE 132.

56

Pete!

"Grrrrrrr!" Pete growls. He laughs. "Fooled you again! But at least you're ready to go."

"Go where?" you grumble. "It's the middle of the night!"

Then you notice that he's holding the map. *Your* map.

"We've got to hurry," Pete tells you. "Look!" He points to some words on the map.

You grab the map from him and frown.

That's funny. Yesterday you couldn't read it at all. But now a few of the words are easy to see.

Maybe some sleep cleared your head.

"'Stand in the doorway of the ruined chapel of San Vicente,'" you read out loud. "'From there you will see a reflection. It comes from the entrance to the Lost Mine.'"

"Cool, huh?" Pete exclaims. "But you can only see the reflection at dawn. We have just enough time."

"But look here," you argue. "The mine entrance is marked. We just have to follow Lost Mine Trail. Why waste time with reflections?"

"I say we find the chapel." Pete folds his arms.

Decide which way to go. It's your map, after all.

To search for the reflection, reflect on PAGE 24.
To take the Lost Mine Trail, trek to PAGE 49.

You decide to jump across the river. You wait for a good gust of wind. There's one now!

You jump as hard as you can!

You soar out over the canyon, gliding along like a bird. Of course you can make it. What were you afraid of?

But then the wind shifts. Just a little.

You start to fall. The dark, foaming river rushes toward you. At the last minute, you spread your paws.

Your flaps are almost like a parachute. But you still hit the water with a splash.

You come up, coughing and gasping for air.

And that's when you start to feel strange. You're changing again! You're growing bigger. The fur on your arms is going away.

You're turning back into a human!

In front of you are the rapids. Jagged rocks, crashing waterfalls, a roar like a jet engine. There's so much foam, you can see why they call it white water.

And you're zooming toward it.

Paddle to PAGE 74.

"What is that?" Pete whispers. "The jawbone of a dinosaur?"

Not quite. But it is a giant set of teeth!

As you get closer, you see that each of the teeth is about two inches long. The whole jaw is about six feet wide. They seem to be made out of some kind of metal.

Carved into the rock wall beside them is this message:

THE WAY TO THE GOLDEN CHAMBER IS DOWN
MY THROAT.

The Golden Chamber? That must be where you'll find the gold!

But you have to go through this giant mouth to get there!

"Those teeth are huge!" Pete says.

"Those aren't teeth," you mutter. "They're some kind of trap."

The teeth suddenly swing shut with a huge *SNAP!*

Go to PAGE 121 — and make it snappy!

Your mind races. You can't figure this puzzle out!

The Watchers step toward you.

"Which of us has the most eyeballs?" the middle Watcher repeats.

"You!" you blurt, pointing to the Watcher on the left.

"Don't be silly," he scoffs. "I sometimes stand in the middle."

The Watcher on the right pipes up, "If he stands in the middle, that means he's standing next to me. And I never stand next to the Watcher with the most eyes. Because I *am* the Watcher with the most eyes!"

He grabs you with a hand made of eyeballs. A hundred eyelashes flicker against your wrist.

"I win!" he shouts gleefully. "And now I get four more!"

"F-f-four more what?" you ask.

"Four more eyeballs!" the creature replies.

You should have seen that answer coming!

Too bad. Next time you take a test, maybe you shouldn't make any more blind guesses!

THE END

You decide to land in front of the tourists. After all you've been through, you might as well have some fun!

You let out a loud "WHO?" as you land on a nearby tree branch. A little girl on the tour gazes up. "Look, Mommy, a big owl."

Hah. That's what *she* thinks.

Just as you land, you feel the change take hold. Your feathers disappear, your wings turn into arms. You're turning into a human before their eyes!

You were right. A thousand heartbeats were up.

The tour group gasps. A few hold up cameras and snap pictures. But most of them are just screaming. In a few more seconds, you turn completely into a person. Cool!

Then you look down and realize you're not wearing any clothes. You're as naked as a jaybird!

Too bad you weren't as wise as an owl when you decided to put on this little show!

THE END

You decide that the Watchers can watch you run!

"Come on, Pete!" you scream. You turn to race toward the entrance.

The sickly light shuts off. You're in total darkness again. You can't see a thing. You can't find the entrance!

You stop dead — and Pete crashes into you. You both sprawl onto the floor.

You hear a squishy sound — like a lot of eyeballs taking a walk. They're coming closer!

And you bet *they* can see in the dark!

Pete grabs your arm. "Which way do we go?" he yelps.

"This way!" you shout, dragging him behind you.

You run flat into a wall. Ouch!

You pull Pete in another direction. Another wall!

The squishy sound comes even closer.

"You didn't even hear the question!" the Watcher complains. It laughs a creepy, nasty laugh. "Prepare yourselves for darkness!"

Cast your eyes on PAGE 109.

It's the snake.

"Um, I just p-p-put your eyes back," you stammer. "Sir."

The snake doesn't say anything. Its empty eye sockets just stare at you.

"So I guess I'll be going now," you babble. You start to move toward the door. A rattle brings you up short.

"Mossst impressive," the snake hisses.

"Excuse me?" you ask.

"Many people have bought my eyesss. And I have hunted them all down. It's lotsssss of fun."

"Glad you enjoyed it," you say.

"But you brought them back yoursssself. Mosssst impressive. Maybe I should give you a pressssent."

You wonder what this snake's idea of a present is. You hope it's not a little love bite and a big squirt of poison.

"How about thissss? You can change into any animal you want for the ressst of your vacation. Does that ssssound like fun?"

Now, *that's* a cool present. Any animal you want! Wait until your older brother hears about this.

Wait a minute. Why should Pete *hear* about this? It will be much more fun to *show* him!

THE END

You've crawled far enough. You're pooped!

You turn around and nervously wait for the other snake.

As he slithers over the dunes, his scales rasp on the sand.

You shiver as he stops in front of you. His tail rises and gives a long rattle.

"Give me back my eyesssss."

You cough up the snake eyes. "Sorry, I was just trying to have some fun," you explain shakily.

"Fun? With someone else's eyes? Hmmph! Well, thanks for finally giving them back, anyway."

He doesn't seem mad. Just happy to have his eyes back. Maybe he's not such a bad snake, after all.

He isn't. In fact, he turns you back into a human. Then he gives you directions to your camp.

While you're walking, you feel something weird in your mouth. Two of your teeth are really sharp!

Whoa! Cool! He let you keep your fangs!

You rub your tongue against them all the way back to camp. You can't wait to smile at your annoying older brother.

You silently send the snake a message: "Fangs for the memories!"

THE END

64

You duck as the shape flies past — as light as a feather.

It's a little white-tailed deer! It prances down the slope.

You burst out laughing. "Nice lion!"

"Oh, shut up," Pete mutters. "Are we there yet?"

You peer at the map. Weird. It seems to be getting even clearer. You can read the whole thing without getting a headache.

And the entrance to the mine is marked as clear as day!

"Look!" You point to a dark cave up on the mountainside. "That's the entrance right there."

"Let's go!" Pete starts to climb toward it.

"Wait!" you shout. "The map says we should go *this* way." You trace a winding path on the map with your finger.

"But we can *see* the entrance!" Pete argues. "Who needs that dumb map? Let's take the short-cut!"

A shortcut would be quicker.

But the map might be magic. Maybe you shouldn't ignore it.

What should you do?

To take Pete's shortcut, turn to PAGE 6.

To follow the map exactly, turn to PAGE 98.

You decide to try to communicate with the ranger. After all, you're smarter than the average bear.

After a moment's thought, you figure out a plan. You can't talk. But you can write.

You walk into the truck's headlights. You reach out with your front leg and try scratching the first letter of your name in the dust. It's hard work. Bear claws weren't made for writing.

But the first letter comes out okay. You start the second.

Then you see another ranger truck pulling up. More rangers are coming.

Better write faster.

Still, it's slow going. Will you make it in time?

If your first name has five letters or fewer, go to PAGE 83.

If your name is longer than five letters, go to PAGE 46.

Your paws slip off the branch, and you drop into the water.

What's happening? you think. I didn't rub the snake eye!

You doggy-paddle as hard as you can. But the current sweeps you into the middle of the river.

The rapids are even closer. And those rocks look sharp!

Then you hear someone calling, "Here, pup! Here, doggy!"

A small inflatable boat comes up behind you. It's full of people with paddles and life jackets. White-water rafters.

You head toward them. They paddle furiously against the current, trying to rescue you before you all hit the rapids.

Just in time, their hands pull your wet dog body onto the boat.

You shake hard, and water flies onto everyone.

"How did a dog get out here?" someone asks.

You try to explain, but all that comes out is a whimper.

"Poor thing. Let's call it Wimpy!"

Wimpy?

There's no time to be annoyed, though. The raft is about to shoot the rapids!

Follow the current to PAGE 85.

You take a step closer to the panther.

It growls and bares its teeth. You break into a cold sweat.

"You're right, Pete," you say. "I'm going for the chest. There's no way I'm letting that panther loose!"

You rush to the chest and pull it away from the wall. You turn the key in the lock, and the lid springs open.

"Pee-yew!" you groan, feeling like you're going to throw up. There's nothing but a lump of smelly meat inside. It must be about a thousand years old!

"Oh, man," Pete moans.

And then —

"GRRR!" The panther snarls. It springs into the treasure chest and starts gnawing at the meat.

In a flash you slam the lid shut and lock it up tight.

"Yes!" Pete yells. "Yes! You did it!"

Your eyes shine with triumph as you scoop up handful after handful of gold. It's all yours!

You're rich!

Looks like this really was a golden opportunity!

THE END

Of course, it wasn't *really* a voice. Just the wind.

You're letting your imagination get carried away.

Besides, you're a bear. Not a chicken.

You keep moving, but the rattle gets closer and closer. When you stop moving, you can hear slithering noises in the dry leaves just behind you. It's a snake all right!

The rasp of its scales almost sounds like whispering. . . .

"Give me back my eyesssss."

The sound sends a chill up your spine.

But this is silly! You're a thousand-pound bear. You're the boss of the forest!

You should face the rattlesnake now, while you're still a mighty bear.

Of course, bears are also good at climbing trees.

The rattle gets closer. What should you do? Turn around and face the snake? Or climb a tree?

To turn around and face the snake, slither to PAGE 92.

To climb a tree, leave this page and go to PAGE 118.

You turn to run.

SNAP!

The teeth grab hold of your shirt!

You pull away. Who cares if you rip a dumb shirt?

But it doesn't help. The teeth only grind up more of the shirt. You're being pulled in — and the teeth are a lot stronger than you.

"Pete! Do something!" you wail.

"Stop it!" Pete shouts. He finds a huge stick and whacks the teeth from behind, over and over again.

They don't stop.

You feel the metal teeth inching up your back.

They start to close around your neck.

Don't panic, you tell yourself. Don't lose your head!

But you have a terrible feeling you're about — *SNAP!*

THE END

You open your mouth to say hello. But when the guards see the eyes, they both let out a yell!

"The crown jewels! You've brought back the crown jewels!"

A crowd surrounds you, and lifts you up on its shoulders.

Soon, you learn the *real* legend of the snake eyes.

It turns out that the jewels belonged to the kangaroo rats long ago. The kangaroo rat queen wore them on her crown. One day, she was snatched away by an evil snake, along with the jewels. They weren't snake eyes after all.

Well, you knew that other legend was just a dumb story.

Magic snake? Hmmph. He was just mean, not to mention eyeless.

For returning the jewels, you are made the ruler of the kangaroo rats!

The problem is, the guard rats lock up the jewels for safekeeping. You can't change back into a human.

But it's nice to be the boss, even if you are a rat!

THE END

"There's no such thing as ghosts!" Pete declares.

"How do you know?" you demand. "The old man at the store said the mine is protected by magic stuff! He said you have to pass a bunch of tests to earn the gold."

"That is so dumb!" Pete rolls his eyes. "I'm going inside to see for myself."

He pushes open the chapel door. "Are you coming?"

To check out the "ghost," go to PAGE 43.
To wait outside for sunrise, go to PAGE 114.

You decide to try feeding the spider.

You reach for Pete's backpack. But the zipper won't open — it's glued shut by strands of the gooey spiderweb!

"Hurry!" Pete yells. He's fighting to loosen the web around his knees.

You give the zipper an extra-hard tug. It opens! You pull two squashed sandwiches out of Pete's backpack.

The spider's snapping jaws are just inches from your face.

"Eeeeaaah!" you scream. You toss a sandwich into the huge mouth. Plastic wrap and all.

"I hope spiders like peanut butter," Pete murmurs.

The spider chews. Swallows.

You throw it your other sandwich. While it chews, you and Pete unwrap your legs. You crawl out of the sticky web.

You're free!

Then you glance up — and gulp.

The spider is done with the sandwiches.

But it looks just as hungry as before!

The next course is on PAGE 38.

Scaring Pete might be fun, but it's just too easy. Besides, you can scare Pete back home, now that you have the power to turn into a bear. You decide to explore the forest instead.

Then you remember what the storekeeper said. If you lose the snake eyes, you can't turn back into a person.

Good thing you remembered! You scoop them into your mouth.

A full moon shines on the forest. In the first few minutes, you spot an owl, a raccoon, and a fox.

And there's nothing to be afraid of, either. You're a bear!

This is going to be the best vacation ever!

You tip your head back, fill your lungs, and let loose a mighty roar. "GRRRRRRAAAAAAAH!"

It was even louder than you thought!

As you listen to the roar echo through the hills, you hear something else. From far away. A rattle. Like a rattlesnake.

The sound makes you think of the legend of the snake eyes. The legend said the magic snake was still searching for its eyes.

But that's just an old story.

Just then, the wind kicks up and whistles through the trees. It almost sounds like a voice. A soft, hissing voice.

"Give me back my eyesssss."

Turn to PAGE 68.

Then you realize something even worse.

In all that coughing and sputtering, you seem to have swallowed one of the snake eyes!

You spit the other one into your hand. Then you feel around your mouth with your tongue.

Yup. It's gone.

But there's no time to worry about that. You're still hurtling toward the rapids.

You look into the remaining snake eye. It's glowing. And it shows a fish. Well, isn't that lucky!

You wonder if fish have trouble with rapids. Instead of changing, you could try swimming for the shore. But the current is so strong.

What's it going to be? Change into a fish, or swim for shore?

To be a fish, flip to PAGE 53.
To try to swim ashore, backstroke to PAGE 78.

You reach over to shake Pete. You gasp.

Pete's sleeping bag is empty. He's gone!

Maybe the thing outside got him!

"Pete?" you whisper again, as loud as you can. Still no answer.

The growl rumbles through the tent again. It's right outside!

You reach for your jeans and pull them on. Your hair feels as if it's standing on end. But you have to help Pete. He may be a pain, but he's still your brother.

Fumbling around in the dark, you manage to find a flashlight. You flip it on and tear open the tent flaps.

You can hardly believe what you see. . . .

Go to PAGE 56.

"That's — that's a panther!" you stammer.

"You said there were no more panthers," Pete objects.

"I guess I was wrong," you admit.

The panther is black and it's huge. It glares at you from inside a cage with golden bars. The cage door is open.

Luckily, though, the panther is chained to the bars. So you feel safe.

Sort of.

"Hey!" Pete nods toward the map in your hand. "It's changing again!"

You spread the map out on the floor. The warning words are finally clear! You and Pete crouch close together to read:

WARNING: DON'T ENTER THE GOLDEN
CHAMBER WITHOUT THE MAGIC KEY!

"Uh-oh. We don't have a key," Pete points out. You keep reading:

A PANTHER GUARDS THE MINE. LIKE ALL CATS,
SHE LOVES TO PLAY WITH HER FOOD.

"What does that mean?" Pete wants to know.

You stare into the panther's green eyes.

There's a hungry expression in them. Very hungry.

To find out what's for dinner, turn to PAGE 125.

The choice is obvious. You go for the map.

If you find all that gold, you can buy a zillion pairs of snake eyes!

You hurry outside and unroll the map. It's full of strange, old-fashioned writing.

The words swim in front of your eyes.

You blink, but it doesn't help.

Hmm. You must still be carsick.

"What's that?" Pete demands, coming up behind you.

"Nothing!" you snap.

"It looks like a map," Pete says. "Can I see?"

"No! Go get your own map!"

"So it *is* a map." Pete grins smugly.

Then he snatches the map from you and runs!

"Hey!" you yell. You chase after him.

Pete suddenly stops short and drops the map.

"Hey! What's that?" he cries.

Find out what Pete is crying about on PAGE 122.

You swim strongly toward the shore. You hope you can make it before you crash into a big rock.

You're a good swimmer. Once you get out of the middle of the river, the current isn't so strong.

The canyon walls are steep, though. There isn't a shore, just a few trees sticking out of the dirt where the walls meet the water. Their branches hang over the river. You reach up and grab one.

All of a sudden your stomach starts to gurgle. As if you are changing again!

But that can't be. You haven't rubbed the snake eye!

Then you realize you haven't eaten for a while. You're hungry. It's just your stomach rumbling.

Phew!

But you're having trouble hanging on to the branch. You peer up at your hand. It's turning into . . . a paw!

You *are* changing again!

You try to yell. But a bark comes out.

Whoa! You're a dog!

Sniff your way to PAGE 66.

Pete lurches at you, waving the railroad spike. He thrusts it between your arm and the metal teeth.

Your shirtsleeve rips in two.

He did it! You're free!

You fall to the ground, rubbing your arm.

It feels like the worst rope-burn in the world.

"Thanks, Pete," you mutter.

"No problem," he answers. "Just call me Dr. Spike!"

The trap makes a loud crunching noise. Then it grinds to a halt. It tried to chew the railroad spike!

"That'll teach you to watch what you eat!" Pete tells it.

For once you don't mind his bad jokes.

You and Pete hurry past the trap and down the tunnel. Then you see light coming through a doorway up ahead.

Golden light!

You and Pete run through the door. You blink in awe.

"We found the treasure!" you cry.

The room is filled with gold. Enough gold to fill a hundred gold mines!

But there's something else too. A pair of green eyes, staring right at you.

Stare back on PAGE 76.

You decide to return the eyes to the shop. You can't keep flying forever. And that snake isn't going to give up.

Just as you reach the shop, you start to feel strange. Queasy.

The thousand heartbeats must be up. You're changing back into a human.

A human with no clothes on.

That's right, you took it all off when you became a bear.

The gift shop isn't open yet, but one of the windows is unlocked. You climb in, trying to be quiet.

The shop is dark, but you find a Lonestar sweatshirt and shorts and pull them on. That's better.

The floorboards creak as you tiptoe across them. You find the dusty old case. You pull open the lid and carefully put the snake eyes back. Well, that should do it. No more magic for you on this vacation.

Then you hear a sound. A slithering sound.

And a rattle fills the dark, empty store.

Turn to PAGE 62.

You wave at the guards and scurry away.

"Come back here!" one shouts.

"Who was that?" the other cries.

You run faster. The guards squeak for help. You hear more rats coming.

You find a long, empty tunnel and rush down it as fast as you can.

But the guards are right behind you.

The tunnel starts to slant upward. Maybe you can make it outside!

Your heart is racing. You must be close to a thousand heartbeats. You'd like to see those guards' faces when you turn back into a human!

But suddenly the tunnel stops. It's a dead end!

Turn to PAGE 137.

You gulp, stepping back toward the stairs.

A low voice cries, "Halt!"

"Do what he says," another voice adds. A shaky voice.

Pete!

You stop. Your eyes slowly adjust to the dark. A figure wearing some kind of old armor looms in front of you.

In one metal-gloved hand, he's holding Pete. In his other hand, he's got a spear — pointed at your chest!

Is that the ghost? You gather all your courage. "Let go of my brother!" you shout.

You swing at the figure's face.

Whoa! There's nothing there! No solid flesh.

The figure really *is* a ghost!

You feel sick.

"Why are you here?" the armor demands. His voice sounds as if it's coming from the bottom of a deep well. "Answer me!"

You open your mouth, but no sound comes out.

"Do something!" Pete cries.

To talk to the ghost, go to PAGE 28.
To run, scram to PAGE 100.

You finish scratching out your name just as two more rangers jump out of their truck.

They both point tranquilizer guns at you.

"Wait," yells the first ranger.

She points to your name in the dust. "This bear can write its name!"

The other rangers gaze at it in wonder.

You sit back and smile. They must think you're the smartest bear in the world.

A big bear-sized truck pulls up, and they open the back. The first ranger points at the ramp.

You decide to obey. You might be a bear, but they've got the guns.

Then, as the truck heads for the ranger station, you remember what the storekeeper said. If you lose the snake eyes while you're an animal, you can't change back into a person.

Uh-oh. They're back at the campsite, lying next to your jeans.

Turn to PAGE 130.

You yell at them to let you go.

"Squawk!"

That didn't sound right. You glance down at your hands, uh, talons. You feel the wind blowing through your shiny black feathers.

You read a sign, hanging at the back of your cage.

You're a raven!

It's not so bad, though. They feed you, water you, and clean out your cage. Too bad those seeds are so tasty! If you could stop eating long enough to get hungry, your stomach would rumble. Then you might change into something that could escape from here.

Ravens can talk, so in the meantime, you're learning a few words.

So far, you can say, "Birdie wants a worm!"

THE END

The boat hits the rapids and crashes into a rock. It tips so far that you almost fall back in the water! But a hand grabs you by the tail. The rafters all grip their paddles.

Another rock looms, but they all paddle furiously. The raft brushes by the rock, spinning to one side. These rafters know what they're doing!

After a while, the wild ride starts to be fun.

Then your stomach rumbles again. You still haven't eaten. And that tingly feeling is coming over you.

Are you changing again?

You remember that you swallowed one of the snake eyes. Maybe your rumbling stomach is *rubbing* the snake eye.

You feel feathers sprout out of your body. Oh, no. You're turning into a bird.

One of the rafters screams! She points and shouts, "Hey! What's happening to Wimpy?"

You must be a terrifying sight. A dog sprouting feathers. What if the rafters get scared and try to hurt you? But right now, the rafters look like your best chance to get home.

Should you fly away, or stay in the boat?

Fly to PAGE 34.
Or stay in the boat on PAGE 52.

It's as if a movie is playing inside the eye!

You see a falcon flying in the moonlight. It circles high above the earth.

You peer into the other eye. This one shows a big black bear, huffing and snorting as it ambles along a hilly trail.

The storekeeper said that if you rubbed the eyes, you would turn into an animal. You're beginning to believe him!

You might as well give it a try.

But which eye should you rub?

What's better: being a falcon or being a bear?

If you want to be a bear, amble to PAGE 32.
If you'd rather be a falcon, fly to PAGE 8.

As you rub the snake eye, you feel yourself stretching and shifting. The muscles in your back grow strong, flexible.

Just before your arms disappear, you pop the eyes into your mouth.

Now you're a snake too! On the sandy ground, you twist and turn until you get the hang of slithering.

Just in time too. You hear the other rattlesnake close behind you.

You snake into the desert. As the sun comes up, the sand is hot on your belly. The wind carries the sound of the snake that's chasing you.

You could swear it's hissing, *"Give me back my eyesssss."*

You crawl on, dune after dune. Your muscles get sore. Maybe you're just not cut out to slither.

Behind you, closer than ever, you hear the other rattler.

Then you see a small fire ahead. Campers! If you can reach them, maybe they'll help you when you turn human again. Or maybe you should just stop running and give that crazy snake its eyes. It's not too late to say you're sorry . . . is it?

To head toward the campfire, slither over to PAGE 107.

To give up the snake eyes, surrender on PAGE 63.

Your fins disappear. Powerful legs replace your tail. And you're getting furry. You're a jackrabbit!

What's going on? You didn't rub the snake eye!

But you can't think about that right now. You have a more urgent problem.

Jackrabbits can't swim very well!

You flail your hind legs, trying to stay above the water. You feel yourself bonk against rocks. You're not a fighter plane anymore, just a wet rabbit in the rapids.

Then your stomach rumbles, and you feel yourself starting to change again.

Why is this happening?

Then you remember that you've got a snake eye in your stomach. Oh, no! Does stomach rumbling count as rubbing the snake eye?

Your nose grows before your eyes. It's turning into some sort of snout!

What now?

Snuffle your way to PAGE 136.

The big cat stares as if it's surprised.

"Smooth move, Pete," you whisper. You're too scared to yell at him.

"Sorry," Pete mumbles in a tiny voice.

The mountain lion jumps to its feet — and leaps away!

You let out a huge sigh of relief. It worked!

"I rule!" Pete yells. "See this hand? This hand threw the rock that destroyed the mountain lion!"

"It almost destroyed *you!*" you snap.

"Says who? Just call me Dr. Rock!" Pete brags. "Lions, and tigers, and bears, beware!" he goes on.

And on, and on — all the way up to the mine.

The entrance is only a small opening, propped up by old wooden beams. You shake the beams. They feel sturdy.

But it's dark inside, and you forgot to bring flashlights.

"Hey, Dr. Rock," you call. "Want to lead the way?"

Pete glances at the dark, forbidding hole. "Dr. Rock says, 'After you.'"

It figures.

Rock on to PAGE 117.

Your heart pounds in your feathered chest as you flap your wings. Why are you changing back so soon? Then you remember: According to the shopkeeper, the transformation only lasts for a thousand heartbeats.

A falcon's heart must beat a lot faster than a human's!

It's a good thing you've still got bird vision. You can see a mountain ledge up ahead. Maybe you can reach it before you lose all your feathers.

There's also a winding river below. Maybe you should head for that. If you turn into a human in midair, the water might break your fall.

To head for the mountain ledge, flap to PAGE 101.

To land in the river, dive to PAGE 37.

You decide to stand your ground. There's no way you can outrun a mountain lion.

You climb up on a rock. Your book said that the bigger you look, the scarier you'll be.

You yell and scream, waving your arms.

"Bad mountain lion! Find somebody else to eat!" you shout.

Pete stares at you as if you're crazy. But he's too tired to run any farther.

The mountain lion pauses for a moment and gazes up at you. It seems confused. Maybe it thinks you're crazy too!

"Go away!" you yell. "You big stupid pussycat!"

The mountain lion sits back on its haunches.

It cocks its head to the side and peers at you.

Is it working? You yell again. "You think you're so tough? Our dog could eat you alive, you dumb lion!"

"Yeah," Pete adds, catching on. "So could our goldfish!"

The big cat sits and licks its paw.

Pete picks up a rock and throws it — hard.

It hits the mountain lion right in the head!

Uh-oh! Your heart suddenly starts to thump faster.

Turn to PAGE 89.

You decide to face the snake. After all, what kind of bear is afraid of a tiny reptile?

You stand in the middle of a clearing, crouched and ready to fight. The rattlesnake slithers out of the forest.

You gulp. The snake isn't tiny. It's about ten feet long. And it's withered and scaly, as if it hasn't shed its skin in a hundred years.

Worst of all, it doesn't have any eyes! Its empty sockets seem to glare menacingly at you.

But you'd better not show it that you're scared. . . .

You stand up and roar. "GRRRRRAAAAAAH!"

As you do, the snake eyes pop out of your mouth onto the ground. And they're glowing! You feel yourself changing.

But you're certain it isn't a thousand heartbeats yet.

Then you realize it wasn't. Because you're not changing into a human. You're shrinking, shrinking . . .

You try to let out another roar.

"CHEEEEEEEP!"

You've turned into a mouse!

Scurry to PAGE 133.

The light from the torches floods the underground chamber. You see more empty suits of armor. Their floating helmets rattle as they turn to stare at you. The torchlight glints red on their swords and spears.

"We have been guarding this passage for four hundred years, waiting for someone to claim the gold," their low, creaky voices moan together.

"Go," the first ghost tells you. "The gold is yours."

A tunnel suddenly appears on your right. It's lined with more flaming torches leading down as far as you can see.

You peer at your map. It doesn't say anything about a secret passage. But then, you still can't make out any of the words. Except one: WARNING.

What if the ghosts are tricking you? Who knows where that passage really leads?

Do you and Pete risk it?

Or do you grab Pete and try to run back upstairs?

To take the passage, go to PAGE 54.
To head back upstairs, go to PAGE 39.

Just as the falcon's claws open over your head, you see a hole in the sand! You dive in. The falcon screeches angrily, and you hear it flap away.

You're in a long tunnel. It's cool down here. Running along, you can smell other kangaroo rats. The smell gets stronger, until a line of rats passes you, chatting about how they need to collect seeds.

Talking rats? Then you remember — you're a rat too. It makes sense that you can understand them.

You pass more rats, digging and carrying things. This must be a kangaroo-rat city! There seem to be miles of tunnels and burrows.

Before long, a huge chamber opens up in front of you. Two guard rats bar the way.

"Why do you want to enter the throne room?" demands one.

"Speak up!" the other one snaps.

If you talk, the guards will see the snake eyes in your mouth. What if they try to take them?

Maybe you should just keep your mouth shut and hop away.

To speak up, go to PAGE 70.

To keep your mouth shut, hop quietly to PAGE 81.

"Gross!" Pete exclaims.

"Do you think those skeletons once belonged to other kids? Kids like us?" you ask fearfully.

"Shhh! Listen!" Pete holds up his hand.

You listen. And you hear a new sound. Some sort of clicking or tapping ahead of you, down the tunnel. It sounds like someone tapping out Morse code.

Hey. Maybe there *is* another kid down here! A live one!

You drag Pete toward the tapping sound.

It gets louder and louder. You go faster.

You race around a turn. And stop short. Staring.

Pete piles into you. "Hey, watch —" he starts to complain.

Then he breaks off. "Whoa," he gasps.

Creeping toward you, clicking its jaws together, is a big spider.

A *really* big spider.

Yikes! Hurry to PAGE 112.

You decide it's time to run like crazy!

Before the ranger can react, you turn and dive into the trees.

Wow! It's like being a tank! You crash through bushes, cactus, and small trees. No way is anyone going to catch you!

After a few minutes of crashing along, you turn around and glance back. Hey! The ranger isn't even trying to follow. You sit down and give a huge roar. "GRRRRAAAAAAAAAH!"

Then you realize that there's a funny feeling in your rear end. A pinprick feeling.

And you're really tired all of a sudden. It almost feels as if . . . you've been tranquilized.

You hear the ranger coming through the trees. But you can't seem to get up.

You start to doze. Then suddenly you remember that there was something important about the snake eyes. What did the storekeeper say? That you weren't supposed to lose them?

Maybe you'll remember once you get some sleep. Yeah, sleep. That's a good idea.

The ranger is coming. Maybe she has a pillow. . . .

There's probably a nice pillow on PAGE 99.

You need to turn into another animal, quick!

You spit the snake eyes out into your palm and gaze at them.

They're glowing! Good!

One shows a small kangaroo rat, hopping along. You once read that kangaroo rats know how to live in the desert. They can even get water from seeds.

The other eye shows a Mojave rattlesnake, slithering along a sand dune. Rattlesnakes are also good at surviving in the desert.

The question is, which animal can escape from that snake that's been stalking you?

You scratch your head, looking back and forth between the snake eyes. A kangaroo rat? They can hop pretty fast.

Or a Mojave rattler? That would put you and the rattler on even footing — or, even stomach — oh, never mind!

You have to choose! You can hear that snake getting closer.

To be a kangaroo rat, jump to PAGE 116.
To be a Mojave rattler, slither to PAGE 87.

"No way am I leaving the trail," you declare.

"You're so lame," Pete jeers.

But he follows you. It takes only a few minutes to reach the mine entrance. The doorway is covered in carved slabs of wood.

"The map says the doorposts contain two special panels." You run your fingers over the wood. "Here they are."

You brush away dust. The panels are made of wood, cracked with age. Each has a strange mark on it.

"What are they for, anyway?" Pete asks.

You read from the map: "'The panel marked with the longer line holds a key inside. Choose!'"

"It's an old trick," you scoff. "The line that looks shorter — the one on the left — is really the longer one."

"Are you sure?" Pete squints. "The one on the right really does look longer to me."

Study them closely. Which is longer?

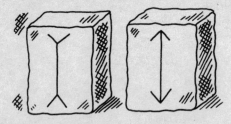

If you think the line on the left is longer, go to PAGE 42.

If you think the line on the right is longer, go to PAGE 108.

You wake up on the floor.

You open your eyes and see thick metal bars.

You're in a cage!

You start to yell, but it comes out as a growl. That's right. You're a bear!

That's when it all comes back to you. The ranger. And the tranquilizer gun.

And the fact that you left the snake eyes lying near your tent.

You curl up and whimper to yourself. You are one sad bear.

It's cold and windy. And a loud noise drones all around you. It sounds like a huge engine.

You see a small window outside your cage. A cloud floats by.

You're on a plane!

Then you remember what happens to troublesome bears in national parks. They ship them off to where they can't hurt anyone. Usually Alaska.

Oh, well. At least you've got a nice warm fur coat!

THE END

100

"Run for it!" you scream, and grab Pete away from the ghost.

You both turn and bolt up the stairs.

The clanking armor is right behind you.

Pete crashes through the old chapel and out the front door onto the dusty street. You follow as best as you can, but you can't help glancing over your shoulder.

The ghost is still running after you! Out here in the red dawn light, he looks even scarier than he did in the dark.

"You cannot escape!" the ghost calls.

You don't like the sound of *that*. You pour on the speed.

But another glance behind shows you that the ghost is catching up to you.

He swipes at you with his spear, tripping you. You crash to the ground.

The ghost stands over you, laughing. "Now you will join us! You will guard the Lost Mine — forever!"

He raises the spear high above you.

Don't get stuck here! Go to PAGE 31.

You flap frantically toward the ledge. As you get closer, you stare cross-eyed at your beak. It's starting to look like a nose. You flap harder, but your wings are turning into arms!

Just as you start to fall, a strong gust of wind pushes you the last few feet to the ledge. You land with a *THUD* on some jagged rocks. Ouch! That hurt — especially since you don't have any clothes on!

You take a deep breath and look around.

There's a cave entrance right in front of you. It's pitch-black. Down below you is a huge canyon, dotted with cactus and tumbleweeds.

The sun is just starting to come up. What a great view!

If you weren't naked, stranded, and freezing, you'd really enjoy it.

And how are you going to get down? It looks like an impossible climb. Impossible for a human being, anyway. . . .

Then you realize the snake eyes are still in your mouth. You spit them into your hand and peer at them. They're glowing!

Take a closer look on PAGE 110.

You and Pete are inside a huge chamber. The murky green light makes it feel as if you're underwater.

But those things in front of you aren't fish. You don't know what they are!

There are three of them. Three huge, bumpy creatures.

You swallow hard. "Be cool," you whisper to Pete.

"S-s-sure," Pete stammers. His eyes are wide in shock.

One of the creatures steps close to you. That's when you realize what all the bumps on it are.

Eyeballs! The creature is made of thousands of eyeballs — all stuck together! Blue, green, brown . . .

Gross!

"We are the Watchers of the Mine!" the creature booms. "We watch for those who want the gold!"

Your mouth is so dry, you can't speak. A sudden chill shakes you. Beside you, Pete gulps.

"To enter the Golden Chamber, you must pass our test," the Watcher continues. "Answer our question correctly, and go forward. Answer wrong — and face the darkness!"

A test! This is what the shopkeeper meant!

Should you take the test? Or run for the door?

To run like crazy, race to PAGE 61.

If you like pop quizzes, take a look at PAGE 19.

The river rushes through the bottom of a deep canyon. It's full of jagged rocks and foaming rapids. No place for a little squirrel. If the wind is just right, maybe you can make it. Maybe.

Once you're on the other side, the snake won't be able to get you, right?

On the other hand, this snake is magic. It seems to be pretty good at keeping up with you.

Maybe you should just give up. You can see the Visitors Center from here. You could soar over and return the magic eyes. Maybe then the snake would leave you alone.

What should you do? Try to cross the raging river or head back to the gift shop at the Visitors Center? Decide quickly. The snake is getting closer. . . .

To try to cross the river, glide to PAGE 57.
To head back to the gift shop, try PAGE 80.

104

You decide to scare Pete. You can't resist! This is your chance to get back at him for all the times he's scared you.

You snuffle at the back of the tent. You hear Pete gasp.

You laugh, but it comes out as a grunt.

It's time to try out your mighty roar. You take a deep breath, sit back on your hind legs, and let loose.

It's so loud and horrible, you almost scare yourself!

Pete runs out of the tent in his pajamas and climbs straight up a tree. He's screaming bloody murder!

You frightened him, all right. Maybe too much. All over the camping ground, you hear people waking up.

So what? They don't scare you. You scare *them*.

You are suddenly lit up by headlights. You turn around. It's a ranger truck.

A ranger gets out. She walks toward you slowly. Is she crazy? You are a mighty bear! And she is a dinky human!

Then you notice that she has a tranquilizer gun. Uh-oh.

Can't bear the suspense? Turn to PAGE 30.

"Wait, Pete! Stop!" you scream. "I'm in the way!"

Pete sees that the car is going to ram into you. He tries to pull it to a stop.

But it's going too fast.

Pete falls to his knees. The car hurtles toward you with sparks flying from its wheels.

You wrench your arm again. But the teeth are holding too tightly onto your sleeve.

"Pete!" you yell. "Do something!"

Pete is speechless. You see his eyes grow wide in horror as the old ore car hurtles straight toward you.

You swallow hard.

So much for your fortune in gold.

This adventure has definitely come off track!

CRASH!

THE END

106

You make a grab for the nearest torch. The trouble is, with your feet all gooed up, you can't quite reach it.

The spider's clicking jaws come even closer.

You throw your whole body at the wall. You did it! You wrap one hand around a torch. "Got it! Pete!" you yell. "Help me!"

Pete lurches against you. His weight knocks you off balance. You pull down on the torch, trying to steady yourself.

The torch squeaks — and moves. It's some kind of lever!

A loud creaking sound drowns out the clicking of the spider's jaws. A hidden panel in the wall slides open.

"A secret passage!" you cheer.

"The spider!" Pete warns. It's almost on top of you!

You manage to yank one foot free from the goo. You kick the spider where its nose should be.

The spider lets out a weird, high-pitched screech. Its huge eyes seem to glow. It scuttles forward.

Great. Before, it was just hungry. Now it's mad!

Quick — turn to PAGE 45.

Slithering into the camp, you spot three people snoozing in sleeping bags. Good. You don't want to scare anybody.

The rattle of the other snake sends a shiver down your spine. And your spine is *long*.

Quick! Where can you hide?

A sleeping bag! The other snake won't look for you there.

You slide in next to a sleeping camper. You peek out.

The other rattler slithers into camp. Then it raises its tail — and rattles!

Two of the campers wake up screaming. They scramble out of their bags. It's almost funny!

But the third one isn't scared. He grabs a long stick with a loop on the end. Like lightning, he whips the loop around the other snake's neck! He stuffs it into a big sack. Yes!

"That'll make a nice belt," he comments.

Then he spots *your* head poking out of the sleeping bag. . . .

Uh-oh! You try to slither away, but he's too fast. In moments, you're dangling from his loop. Trapped.

"This one'll make an excellent purse!" he exclaims.

A purse! How embarrassing!

You thought this adventure would be cool. But now, don't you wish you could just bag it?

THE END

You stare at the panels. Then you push the right-hand one.

It slides open! A small golden key glows inside.

Amazing! Pete was right!

"Yes! Yes! I don't know why everyone thinks *you're* the smart one," Pete crows. "Just call me Einstein!"

You ignore him and grab the key.

It starts to glow!

Holding the key in front of you, you step inside the entrance. An old railroad track leads into darkness.

You follow the track by the key's glow. It's tough going.

It's also dusty — and Pete starts sneezing. "ACHOOOO!"

"Shhhh!" you hiss.

"Who's going to hear us? Monsters?" Pete teases.

"Quit it," you mutter. "I know there aren't such things as monsters."

Then you see something gleaming in the light from the key.

Teeth. Monstrously big teeth!

"A m-monster!" Pete yells, turning to run.

Chew on PAGE 36.

You drop to the ground. Your hands scrabble in loose dirt.

"Pete — the dirt!" you yell. You scoop up a handful and throw it toward the Watcher.

"Ouch!" the creature yells.

You heave another handful of dirt. Another.

Then your fingers scrape rock. You whirl around, feeling for more dirt — and spy a yellow light shining up ahead.

"This way!" you yell.

You grab Pete's hand and stumble into a narrow passage lit by torches.

For some reason, the Watchers don't follow.

You soon realize why.

The floor of the tunnel is completely covered with broken skeletons. The skeletons are covered with some sort of nasty, sticky goo.

Follow your own eyeballs to PAGE 95.

You hold up one of the eyes. You can see a tawny, muscular mountain lion in it. Hey! *Mountain* lions don't have trouble climbing down mountains, you think.

You gaze into the other eye. It shows a bat, flitting through a dark sky. You shiver. You have had enough flying for one day.

On the other hand, bats can see in the dark. You could explore the cave in front of you, and then climb down. After all, this *is* supposed to be a fun vacation.

What'll it be? Should you try to climb down as a mountain lion or explore the cave as a bat?

To become a bat, turn to PAGE 12.
To become a mountain lion, turn to PAGE 35.

You hold out the glowing key. You're afraid of what you might see. Pete's not the best brother in the world, but it's better to have one whole brother than two half brothers.

But Pete is on the other side of the trap. Grinning!

He pumps his fist into the air. "I made it!"

You stare at the stick in the trap — or what's left of it. The trap splintered it!

A second later the trap groans and resets itself.

"Your turn!" Pete yells. "Come on, chicken! It's easy. It's all in the timing."

You don't know what to do. Pete made it past. But you're not Pete. Should you try to jump through the trap?

Or is there another way?

"Bawk! Bawk! Bawk!" Pete yells, flapping his arms.

To jump through the trap, hurl yourself at PAGE 11.

To find another way, take a peck — uh, peek — at PAGE 50.

The spider's eight huge eyes glisten in the torchlight. Its body is the size of a small car and covered with thick hair.

And it's getting closer.

"Let's get out of here!" Pete yells.

You and Pete turn to run. But somehow, your legs get all tangled up.

You fall over — and Pete falls with you.

"Run!" Pete screams.

"I *was* running!" you yell, trying to untangle yourself from him. But you seem to be stuck.

You peer down at your legs. A mass of white goo covers them.

It's hard, but you pull yourself free. You lean over to help Pete. Then you catch movement out of the corner of your eye. A long, slender thread shoots out of the spider's mouth.

More goo!

"It's wrapping us up like flies!" you whisper in horror as the goo winds around your legs. You can't move them!

But you can move your eyes to PAGE 127.

You are hungry. And that worm looks good.

Then you realize what you're thinking. I want to eat a worm. Yuck!

But, hey, the next time your stomach rumbles, you could turn into a worm. And you'd rather eat one than *be* one.

You swoop up toward the wriggling worm.

And swallow it whole!

As you gulp it down, you try to imagine a nice ham sandwich. And you try not to feel it give a final wiggle.

Why is a worm in the water, anyway? you think. Stupid worm.

Then you feel something sharp in your mouth.

A hook!

As you get yanked out of the water, you have another thought.

I should have known that worm looked fishy. . . .

THE END

"I'm waiting right here for sunrise," you declare.

The moan comes from the old chapel again.

To your surprise, Pete stops in his tracks.

"Hah! So you're scared after all!" you crow.

"I am not," Pete insists. "I just don't want to miss the sunrise."

The sun slowly climbs in the sky. Across the desert, you begin to see the faint outline of a huge mountain.

"I don't see any reflection," Pete complains. "This was a stupid waste of time!"

"Oh, yeah?" you reply. "What about *that*?"

On the mountain, something that looks like the entrance to a cave suddenly glows. The light gets brighter and brighter, shining straight into your eyes!

"The Lost Mine!" you whoop with excitement.

"Let's go!" Pete exclaims.

You stare at the land between you and the mountain. It looks like dangerous territory — dotted with jagged cliffs and sharp-edged canyons. One wrong step, and . . .

You take a deep breath. "Great," you mutter. "How do we get there — alive?"

Exhale and turn to PAGE 10.

The green glow fades. A pale golden light takes its place. It reveals a rocky tunnel.

"I guess we follow the gold light," you murmur.

Pete shrugs. "Hey, you're the smart one."

You make your way down the tunnel. The air is cold and clammy. But the golden light seems to be getting brighter.

You glance down. The key in your pocket is glowing! The glow grows stronger with every step you take.

"We must be getting closer to the Golden Chamber," you tell Pete. Your heart thumps with excitement.

You and Pete follow the tunnel around a sharp turn.

"Yeow!" you cry. The light is so bright, it hurts!

You drop back into the tunnel.

"The Golden Chamber!" Pete cries. He runs past you into the bright room.

"Pete, wait!" you shout. "It *can't* be this easy to get the gold!"

"Sure it — " Pete's voice suddenly stops.

"Pete?" you call. But he doesn't answer.

Then you hear it.

It's kind of a nice sound. Almost like a cat purring.

A very *big* cat.

Shhh! Turn noiselessly to PAGE 13.

Rats! That's the ticket. You rub the eye and start to shrink. You pop the snake eyes into your mouth. Soon you have whiskers, a long tail, and powerful hind legs.

The hiss of a rattlesnake comes from a few feet away. Whirling around, you spot it.

The snake's long brown body slides and bumps through the rocks. Its forked tongue flickers in and out of its cruel mouth. And its eyes! Its eyes are nothing but gaping sockets, with raw flesh oozing out of them.

Your whiskers twitch, and you squeak with fear!

The snake suddenly coils and rears up!

You hop away so quickly, you're almost flying! You try to count your heartbeats, but they're coming way too fast. Still, you're putting a lot of distance between you and the snake.

Soon another sound makes your rat ears perk up. It's a screeching — coming from above. You peer into the sky.

A falcon is circling overhead!

You remember how good your eyesight was when you were a falcon. And to the falcon, you probably look like lunch.

You hop like crazy, but the screeching comes closer, and you hear wings flapping just over your head!

Hop faster! To PAGE 94.

You lead Pete into the mine. Bat wings flutter overhead. After walking all that way in the bright sun, you can hardly see in here.

You feel your way down a long tunnel. "Ow!" you mutter as you bang your shins on some kind of metal cart.

You peer at it in the gloom. It looks like an old ore car.

"Hey — didn't these old cars run along railroad tracks?" Pete asks.

"Yeah," you answer. You stoop down and feel tracks on the ground. "And that means we can follow these tracks — maybe right to the gold!"

You and Pete kick your feet alongside the tracks to find your way. You wave your arms around in front of your faces, to keep from walking into anything.

You squint into the darkness. Is that a light up ahead?

"Pete!" you exclaim. "I think I see something!"

You hurry closer. And a cold chill shakes you.

You don't like what you see.

Take a closer look on PAGE 58.

Maybe climbing a tree is safer. After all, rattlesnakes can't climb trees. Can they?

You pick a tall oak tree and start clawing your way up the trunk.

Just in time. The snake slides into view below.

A chill goes up your spine. The snake's scales are old and withered. It makes a dry sound on the leaves as it crawls.

As the snake curls around the tree trunk, you notice something horrifying.

The snake's eye sockets are deep, black, and empty! How does it see? you think. How did it find me?

It raises its tail. Rattle! RATTLE!

The wind picks up in the trees. The branch you're on starts to shake. The blowing leaves seem to hiss the words.

"Give me back my eyesssss."

You howl with fear.

Then you hear a buzzing sound. Black shapes begin to flit in front of your eyes.

You glance up.

On the branch above you is a bees' nest.

Uh-oh.

Buzz your way to PAGE 48.

You sail through the air, still holding the stick in front of you.

But the jaws don't bite.

Not yet, that is.

As you hurtle into the rusty teeth, the trap almost seems to be smiling.

Well, why shouldn't it smile?

You're probably pretty tasty.

THE END

You decide to change into a hummingbird. As you rub the eye, you feel feathers sprouting out all over your body.

You gasp as your arms turn into wings, and you drop the snake eyes. You flutter your tiny, rainbow-shiny wings. They beat so fast, you can hardly see them out of the corner of your eye.

You look down and see your feet turning into claws. You swoop to the ground to grab the snake eyes.

But the eyes are too big for your itsy-bitsy bird feet! You try to hold on, but they fall to the ground. The snake hisses with delight. It crawls away with the eyes.

What's wrong with this picture? You've got hummingbird feet and hummingbird wings, but you still have a small human body.

You're half-person, half-bird!

You must have dropped the eyes before changing all the way into a bird. What did the storekeeper say? Don't lose the eyes, or you won't be able to change back.

You're stuck this way!

You flap along, trying to follow the snake. But you can't really fly that well.

"Wait!" you cry. "Just let me change back into a person!"

But the snake slithers into the bushes.

Oh, well, there's always a career in the circus. . . .

THE END

You jump back, but not fast enough.

The trap catches the sleeve of your shirt!

"What happened?" Pete yells.

"It got my sleeve!" You pull as hard as you can, but your sleeve won't come free.

Then you hear a screeching noise.

The teeth are moving!

They're grinding together. Your sleeve is slowly being pulled into the trap.

And your arm is being pulled closer to the teeth.

"It's trying to eat me!" you scream. "Pete, find something sharp! Try to cut my sleeve off!"

Pete hesitates. "Or maybe I could push the old ore car into the trap," he says. "And smash it to bits!"

This is no time to argue! Decide what to do.

Tell Pete to find something sharp on PAGE 23.

Tell him to crash the ore car into the trap on PAGE 27.

You scoop the map off the ground. There's a word at the bottom that you didn't see before.

WARNING!

It's printed in big red letters. They're dripping down the page. Like blood!

"What kind of map is that?" Pete demands.

You're too shocked to answer. You shake your head to clear your vision.

When you examine the map again, the blood is gone.

So is the rest of the warning.

Weird.

Your parents come out of the Visitors Center. "Time to set up camp," your dad calls.

You stick the map in your pocket. You're glad to put it away.

That night, you dream about panthers and bears. You wake with a start in the tent you share with Pete. It's very dark.

SCRITCH! GRRRRRR!

There's something outside!

"Pete! Did you hear that? Pete!" you whisper.

Pete doesn't answer.

Then you hear a growl.

Don't just lie there. Turn to PAGE 75.

You shrink back. You close your eyes.

This is it, you think. You brace yourself for the feel of those razor-sharp claws.

Nothing happens.

Your eyes fly open. The panther jerks to a stop in midair and drops to the ground.

Aha! Its golden collar is attached to a long golden chain. The panther can't move any farther.

It can't reach you!

"Phew!" you gasp. Your heart starts beating again.

The panther curls up, never taking its eyes off you.

"Hey," Pete whispers behind you. "Look at the map!"

You glance down. The rolled-up map is glowing!

You pull it out of your pocket and stare at the bright red letters:

WARNING!

The words underneath are suddenly crisp and clear.

Be warned on PAGE 7.

Scaring the tour group would be fun. But you've had enough "fun" for one day. You head for your campsite.

You land behind your tent. No one seems to be awake. Good.

Your feathers start to disappear. And your wings are turning into . . . arms! All right. It's good to be human again.

You find your jeans and pajama top right where you left them. As you pull them on, your stomach starts to rumble. You'd better eat something, fast!

You find your dad's keys and open the bear-proof food locker. The first thing you see is a loaf of bread. You gobble down a piece. There's some turkey, so you grab a handful of that.

Then you make yourself a peanut butter sandwich. Then you make another.

When your family gets up, you're still eating.

"For heaven's sake," your mom yells, "you've eaten half the food!"

"Better get more." Your words are muffled by the food in your mouth. But your mother will understand soon enough.

You've *got* to keep eating. One stomach rumble and you could become a dinosaur, or a lizard, or an ant!

You're going to be fat pretty soon. But at least you'll never be hungry again!

THE END

"I guess we need the key to lock that panther in its cage," you say. "Maybe we should go back and see if we can find it."

"No way! Who cares about the panther?" Pete swaggers toward the gold. "It's chained! It can't reach us."

"Uh, Pete, . . ." you begin. "I think that depends on the length of the chain."

"Well, how long is this one, genius?" Pete asks.

Before you can answer, the panther leaps toward you.

You have just enough time to notice that the chain is *very* long.

You'd like to draw a diagram for Pete.

But it's awfully dark inside a panther's mouth. . . .

THE END

126

The entrance doesn't look like you thought it would. It's just a deep, dark cave, choked with weeds and bushes. It's also wide open. Anyone could find it.

Even Pete notices. "This is it?" he asks. "Are you sure you read the map right?"

"Yes, I read the map right!" You peer into the cave. It seems to lead to a tunnel.

You have that bad feeling again. It's all been too easy. Could it be a trick?

"So, I guess we go inside," you say. You try to act braver than you feel.

You push past the bushes and duck into the cave. It's pitch dark in there.

Pete bumps into you from behind. "Sorry," he mutters.

You walk forward carefully. "I can't believe we forgot flashlights," you complain.

"That won't be necessary," a deep voice booms out.

A sickly green glow suddenly lights up the cave. It's just bright enough for you to see where the voice came from.

You stare in horror.

You *knew* this was too easy!

It gets harder on PAGE 102.

You and Pete are caught — like flies in a spider-web.

The spider crawls even closer. It's gigantic!

"How did it get so big?" Pete whispers.

"I don't know!" you snap. "Maybe it's been down here for hundreds of years, eating."

"Eating?" Pete echoes. "Uh-oh."

You both stare at the broken bones under your feet. You have a feeling you just found out what happened to those people!

"We have to do something," you declare. "Hey! The sandwiches!"

"How can you think of food now?" Pete exclaims.

"Not for me, for the spider!" you cry. "Throw it the sandwiches we packed! Then it won't need to eat *us!*"

"Those tiny sandwiches? That spider is giant!" Pete argues. "Let's try to get one of those torches off the wall. Maybe it's afraid of fire!"

If you want to grab a torch, turn to PAGE 106.
If you feed the spider your sandwiches, go to PAGE 72.

128

You've got it! You've figured out the answer!

"The one with the most eyes is you!" you shout, pointing to the creature on the right.

The middle Watcher blinks all his eyeballs at once. "That's right," he grumbles. "How did you know?"

You try to explain. "Well, the Watcher on the right said he never stands next to the Watcher with the most eyes. But he's standing next to you, since you're in the middle. And he has to stand next to the Watcher on the left when the Watcher on the left stands in the middle. The only Watcher he never stands next to is himself. So he must be the Watcher with the most eyes!"

"Huh?" Pete murmurs.

"Congratulations. You passed. Now take your prize!" The Watcher in the middle holds out a small golden key.

"Oh — and beware the panther," he adds.

The Watchers turn and squish into darkness.

"Wait!" you call. "What panther! And what is the key for?"

"Follow the gold and find out!" one Watcher replies.

Gold? What gold?

Find out what they mean on PAGE 115.

Suddenly, the wind catches your little flaps. One moment you're falling.

The next moment you're . . . swooping!

You zoom over the snake. "See you later, distant relative of the alligator!" you shout. But it sounds more like a cheep.

You land on the next tree. That was easy! More importantly, that was *fun*.

You launch yourself again. This time, you catch the wind right away and you glide farther. You're getting good at this!

But as you fly from tree to tree, you notice something.

No matter how far you go, you can still hear the snake behind you.

Snakes should crawl much slower than flying squirrels, right?

"Give me back my eyesssss."

You jump again. You soar to the next tree.

But when you land, you realize you're in trouble. There's a huge river between you and the next bunch of trees.

It's farther than any jump you've made so far.

Much farther. And the rattler sounds closer than ever.

Soar to PAGE 103.

You're stuck as a bear!

But being a bear isn't too bad.

Especially when you're the smartest bear in the world.

A lot of scientists come to watch you write your name. They ask you questions about what it's like to be a bear.

Writing long answers is hard work, but it makes them happy.

And when they're happy, they give you honey. Mmmm.

And raw fish. And nuts and berries.

And mice. You love those teeny, tasty morsels!

Plus you get to sleep all winter. No more going to school on dark, freezing-cold mornings!

Yup. It's a pretty good life.

And since you're stuck this way, you might as well . . . grin and bear it!

THE END

You flap your wings like crazy. You feel yourself lift into the air. You open your eyes — your campsite is yards below you.

You realize there's *nothing* holding you up. For a second, you have a sick, sinking feeling. You're falling!

Then your wings stretch out and catch the air. Instead of falling, you're soaring! Up, up, up!

The tents and your parents' car are so far below, they look like toys. But with your keen falcon's eyesight, you can make out every detail.

You wing along through the crisp night air. It's amazing. It's awesome. You're really flying!

All of a sudden, that funny tingling in your stomach comes back.

Uh-oh.

You're turning back into a human.

And you're about a mile above the ground.

Now what?

Find out on PAGE 90.

You duck and hold your breath.

CRASH!

When you open your eyes, you find yourself on the ground. You must have been thrown out of the car. There's dust everywhere.

Then you realize that the snake eyes flew out of your hand! You search for them on hands and knees.

Unfortunately, it's too dark to see anything so small in this tunnel.

But what you do find makes you gasp. Bones! Human bones. You're gazing straight into the eyes of a skull when you hear a sound.

Through the gloom, a figure is shambling down the tunnel toward you. It walks like some sort of evil robot! Stumbling and tripping on the bones.

You try to find a place to hide, but there's nowhere to run. And when you see the face of the figure, you scream!

Turn to PAGE 14.

A mouse? How could this be happening?

You scurry to the snake eyes and rub them with your little paws. You don't even bother to peer into them. Anything would be better than being a mouse.

That's because mice are high on the list of a snake's favorite food. . . .

You keep rubbing the eyes frantically. But no matter how hard you rub, nothing happens.

The snake slithers over to you.

"Those are *my* eyessss, remember?" it hisses. "I control them. And I can change you into anything I pleassse."

Uh-oh. You never thought of that.

You try to explain that you were just having some fun. But all that comes out are little cheeps.

The snake hisses hungrily. . . .

As you look at its looooong body, you realize it will take you a while to reach

THE END.

Maybe it's time to get going.

You leap down the mountain, jumping from rock to rock. Even deep clefts don't slow you down. You jump right over them.

Finally you stop to rest.

Your sharp mountain lion ears pick up a slithering sound behind you. The snake!

But that can't be! How could a snake slither fast enough to keep up with a mountain lion!

Then you hear a rattle echoing through the rocks. Your fur stands on end.

You have to keep moving.

You lunge down the mountainside.

Then, with only a few more leaps to the desert floor, you get a queasy feeling.

A thousand heartbeats must be up. You're starting to change!

You speed up. But just as you're jumping toward a stony ledge, you see your claws turning back into hands!

You just reach the ledge. You grab at it with your hands. But you can't hold on! You're slipping. . . .

Get a grip on PAGE 40.

It says: WARNING! These eyes were stolen from a magic rattlesnake. . . .

Pete yanks the paper from your hand. He reads in a low voice that's supposed to sound scary.

"'The snake could turn into any animal — with a blink of its magic eyes.' Oooooh, I'm scared!" Pete wails.

"Give that back," you shout, grabbing for the paper.

Pete whips it away and keeps reading. "'It could become a field mouse and crawl through the smallest hole. It could see for miles with the sharp eyes of an owl.' This is *so* dorky."

"Shut up, Pete!" you yell. "Give it back."

"Wait! It gets better." He laughs and keeps reading. "'One day, a brave eagle plucked out the snake's eyes. He gave them to the Quezot Indians. For centuries, the Quezot used the eyes to change themselves into animals. Now *you* have the power to transform yourself. But the magic carries a price.'"

Turn to PAGE 33.

Your skin is getting bristly. Your snout gets longer. You are turning into some kind of pig!

Then you remember your books. There's a creature in these parts called a javelina. It's a kind of wild pig.

Unfortunately, javelinas can't swim any better than rabbits. Bonk! You bounce off another rock.

Plus you're still hungry. You feel your stomach rumble again. Then the tingly feeling comes over you.

This is bad. The snake eye in your stomach is changing you every time it moves around in there!

Scales suddenly pop out of your arms. You gasp for air, and find that you've got gills again. You're a fish!

Maybe you should head for shore. Before your growling stomach changes you into something else that can't swim.

Or maybe you should eat a fish dinner. You've got to stop your stomach from rumbling.

You see a minnow flit by in front of you. Or — there's a nice patch of algae by the bank. And a worm is wiggling above you on the surface — a fat, juicy worm.

Well?

Head for shore on PAGE 9.
Chow down on PAGE 113.

The guards close in, and you cough out the snake eyes. Maybe you can turn into something bigger!

But the eyes aren't glowing! When you look into them, you don't see a thing. You're trapped.

One of the guards sees the snake eyes. "You've got the crown jewels!" he screeches. "You must be the one who stole them!"

The other rats crowd around, squeaking and climbing over each other.

"Wait a minute! These are snake eyes! From the store —" you protest.

"Of course they are!" snaps the first guard. "But they're also our crown jewels. You'll see why when you meet our king!"

They drag you back to the throne room and wait for the king to return.

You hear him coming long before he arrives. Your sensitive ears pick up the slither of his scales in the dirt tunnel. It's the rattlesnake!

King Rattlesnake, that is!

THE END

About R.L. Stine

R.L. Stine is the most popular author in America. He is the creator of the *Goosebumps*, *Give Yourself Goosebumps*, *Fear Street*, and *Ghosts of Fear Street* series, among other popular books. He has written more than 100 scary novels for kids. Bob lives in New York City with his wife, Jane, teenage son, Matt, and dog, Nadine.